THE REAL
PLATO JONES

THE REAL
PLATO JONES
by Nina Bawden

CLARION BOOKS / *New York*

Clarion Books
a Houghton Mifflin Company imprint
215 Park Avenue South, New York, NY 10003
Text copyright © 1993 by Nina Bawden

Library of Congress Cataloging-in-Publication Data

Bawden, Nina, 1925–
    The real Plato Jones / by Nina Bawden.
        p.   cm.
    Summary: Thirteen-year-old Plato Jones tries to come to terms with
his mixed heritage while visiting Greece, as he finds out more about
his Welsh grandfather, a World War II hero, and his Greek
grandfather, a supposed traitor.
    ISBN 0-395-66972-3
    [1. Greece—Fiction.   2. Grandfathers—Fiction.   3. World War,
1939–1945—Greece—Fiction.   4. Identity—Fiction.]   I. Title.
PZ7.B33Rc   1993
[Fic]—dc20   92-43873
                                                        CIP
                                                        AC

AGM   10   9   8   7   6   5   4   3   2   1

To Annie and Michael Sumner

Novels for Young Readers by Nina Bawden

Carrie's War
Devil by the Sea
The Finding
A Handful of Thieves
Henry
The House of Secrets
Humbug
Kept in the Dark
The Outside Child
The Peppermint Pig
Rebel on a Rock
The Robbers
The Runaway Summer
Squib
Three on the Run
The White Horse Gang
The Witch's Daughter

THE REAL
PLATO JONES

⊛CHAPTER·1

My name is Plato Jones. Plato Constantine Jones. Plato because my mother is Greek, and Jones because my father is Welsh, and Constantine after *his* father, my grandfather, who is Constantine Llewellyn Jones. AKA CLJ. AKA Jones-the-Spy.

Most people call my grandfather CLJ, even his family. But in the Welsh valley where he lives with my grandmother and my Uncle Emlyn, there are so many Joneses that they have to be set apart from each other. The postman is Jones-the-Post, the fishmonger Jones-the-Fish, and my Uncle Emlyn, who is a teacher, is Jones-the-School. So my grandfather has to be Jones-the-Spy. In the valley they don't take any special notice of anyone famous.

And CLJ is famous. He is a real hero, part of history like Julius Caesar or Robin Hood or George Washington. The only difference is that CLJ is still alive and so you can see him on television.

He is famous because of the Second World War. That was the war that England and America and Russia and most of the other countries in Europe fought against Hitler's Germany way back in the forties. Before this war, CLJ had taught classics at Oxford University, and because he could speak modern Greek he was dropped by parachute into Greece to help organize the Greek Resistance against the Germans. The Greeks were good guerrilla fighters but they were short of radio equipment and weapons. CLJ lived with a group of guerrillas in a cave in the mountains, and used his radio to tell the commander-in-chief of the Allied forces where to drop the guns and explosives they needed to blow up roads and bridges to cut the German army's supply lines.

My father says all CLJ ever told him about what he did in the war was that he was cold most of the time and hungry most of the time and frightened all of the time. But my father says that was just CLJ's way of telling him that war is a mug's game and to be avoided if possible. Even when it was over and CLJ got all his medals for bravery, he wasn't proud; he just shoveled them away in a drawer as if the idea of being picked out and decorated as a brave man was embarrassing to him.

CLJ lived with the Resistance for over a year. The village below the cave was occupied by the Germans, but the Greeks who still lived there, the old men and the women and children, brought food and water and news whenever they could, pretending that they were herding their goats to a higher pasture or taking a donkey to pick up some firewood. The Germans knew about CLJ by this time and had offered a reward for his capture. And in the end one of the villagers told the German commandant where he was hiding and he had to run for his life. He only escaped because a girl came to warn him; she led him over the mountains to the town of Iria, on the coast, and hid him in a cellar until the Royal Navy sent a submarine to pick him up late one night.

◆

This is how I come to be half Greek and half English. The girl who rescued CLJ was my mother's Aunt Elena. And thirty years or so later, when my father was in Athens on a business trip, he took a few days' holiday and went to Iria, to visit Elena. And while he was there he met her niece, Maria Petropoulos, and fell in love with her.

◆

The Second World War is ancient history now. Fifty years ago. But the way my Welsh grandmother carries on, it might have been yesterday. Although it was a Greek girl who saved CLJ, my grandmother decided long ago that she hated all Greeks because it was a Greek who had betrayed him in the first place. "No good asking me to forgive them," she says. As if anyone would dare! "As for *you*," she hisses, stabbing me with a specially venomous look, "if CLJ had been shot by the Germans, where d'you think *you'd* be?"

"I don't know," I usually answer, looking as po-faced as I can manage. "You tell me."

That fixes her. "Your father wasn't born when CLJ went to Greece and I wasn't pregnant either" is the obvious reply but she can't get her tongue around it. Or not in front of me. Even though she must know that a boy of thirteen and a half is likely to know the facts of life. Of course people of her great age are bound to be a bit inhibited about sex, though

[3]

the point she was trying to make had rather more to do with biology.

I think she must always have hated my mother for having the cheek to marry my father in the first place. Not that she was ever foul to her, not when I was around anyway, but when my father went off and left us, my grandmother didn't pretend to be sorry. My sister, Aliki, decided to live with our father and his new wife in New York and my grandmother put on a great act of amazement when she heard that I didn't want to. "You'd think you'd want to be with your little sister," she said.

"Oh, I'd like to be with *Aliki*, all right," I told her meaningfully. Did she really think I wanted to *talk* to my father, let alone live with him, after what he had done?

And even leaving that out of it, *someone* had to stay in England to look after my mother. My grandmother ought to have known that better than anyone. She was always telling my father how useless my mother was at just about everything. Naturally, she put it down to her being Greek. Or not being Welsh, anyway. Perhaps if my mother had been English, or even Irish or French or Italian, my grandmother would have found it just about bearable, but to be Greek was the worst fate she could think of.

And not only for my mother. It really *pains* my grandmother when she is forced to contemplate the harsh fact that her grandchildren have Greek blood in their veins. If I wave my hands about, or sound excited, or do anything that she disapproves of, she says, "That's the Greek in you, Plato," and sighs as if this is a truly dreadful burden to carry. (What she would do if I spat or held up five fingers to ward off the evil eye defeats my imagination.)

[4]

There was a time when I think my Welsh grandmother would have liked to suggest that it was my Greek ancestry that made me small for my age and boss-eyed and asthmatic, but she never quite dared. Both she and CLJ come from Welsh mining families and are short for grown-ups, and although Uncle Emlyn has never been down a mine you can hear the dusty wheeze in his chest half a street away, and my father wears heavy-lensed glasses like mine. But she does say things like, "I don't think you've put on an ounce since I last saw you, Plato. I suppose it must be all that foreign food your mother cooks for you."

If Uncle Emlyn hears her make this kind of remark he winks at me and shrugs his shoulders. He never answers his mother back any more than my father does. My Welsh grandmother is a tiny woman with hunched shoulders and a little, beaky-nosed face like a baby owl, but those two grown men are scared stiff of her.

I don't think CLJ can be scared, not with all his medals for bravery, but he doesn't answer back either. Perhaps that is because he almost never hears her. "Deaf as a post," she says, although I have heard Uncle Emlyn talking quite normally to him when she isn't around. CLJ does have a hearing aid, but he only uses it on special occasions: when he has to make a speech in public or be interviewed on television. He never wears it at home.

"Being deaf is the only protection he's got, poor unfortunate man," my mother says.

She is just as uncharitable about my grandmother as my grandmother is about her. My mother doesn't care for the Welsh people very much. She says you can't trust them and they are stupid to make so much fuss about their boring old language. Welsh isn't like Greek, which is the language of a noble and ancient culture. The Greeks were building great cities and temples and writing great plays for their theaters while the Welsh were still grunting away at one another like illiterate monkeys.

◆

When my mother goes on like that I want to stand up for the Welsh, just as when my grandmother carries on about how awful Greeks are I want to stand up for *them*. It's being half-and-half myself, I suppose. Half Greek and half Welsh-and-English—after all, I live most of the time with my mother in England, and I can't see so much difference be-tween the people in our town near London and those in my grandparents' village in Wales. When I'm in Wales or in England I often feel very Greek. I think how funny and shut away these people are, living their indoor lives behind closed doors and curtains. And when I'm in Greece I sometimes think there is quite a lot to be said for being private and keeping your true feelings hidden.

◆

Take my grandfather's funeral. My mother's father, that is, my Greek grandfather. Name of Nikos Petropoulos. That was a pretty discommunious affair, I can tell you. Or as some people might say, discombobulating.

My mother had a telephone call on the Friday night. I was doing my homework (a stupid history essay on how it might have felt to live through the Great Plague, a piece of cake for someone of even my minuscule mental abilities)

[6]

when I heard her squealing in the hall. She was squealing in Greek, so I couldn't understand more than a word or two. (If I started to learn Greek I'd have to learn Welsh as well or my grandmother would raise the roof. So I just say I'm bad at languages. It's probably true, anyway.)

But although I didn't understand what my mother was saying, I knew something had happened by the dramatic tone and the volume. I reckoned she could have been heard in Athens even if Alexander Graham Bell had never invented the telephone. And by the time I got to her she was howling.

She had put the receiver down and was leaning against the wall, her knees sagging and tears running down her face like rain down a window. She said, "It's my father, oh Papa, oh Plato . . ."

And then she went on in Greek, which was a relief in one way; it meant that I could get on with the things that had to be done without having to pretend I was paying attention. I sat her down in the sitting room and turned off the television and made her a cup of tea. I rang Olympic Airways and fixed a booking for Saturday, on the lunchtime flight, and said we would pick the tickets up at the airport. I rang my father in New York and luckily got him and not his wife, whom I don't care to speak to if I can avoid it, and said if he could come with Aliki on the flight from New York we could meet them in Athens.

If this makes me sound unnaturally efficient and bossy for a person my age, I can only say that I had been looking after my mother for two years by this time and had got fairly well used to my role in her life. And I knew that if her father was definitely dying there was no time to waste if she was to get to the funeral. When a Greek dies they try to bury him the next day, and Nikos Petropoulos lived in a mountain village a long way from the airport.

By the time I had made these two telephone calls she was calmer. She had finished her tea and poured herself a gin and tonic. "Just to steady me, Plato," she said, rolling her eyes and giving me a bit of a grin, sly or shy, I wasn't sure which. She'd had two gins before supper but it didn't seem quite the moment to start acting like the man from Alcoholics Anonymous.

I said, "I suppose hearing your father is dying is as good an excuse as any for hitting the bottle."

I never know whether it's best to make jokes about something serious or pull a long face. It's usually safer to make jokes. Certainly, in this case she smiled quite cheerfully and took a good swig of her gin before putting the glass down and looking mournful again.

"Oh, Plato," she said, "d'you think we'll get there *in time?* It's been so long since I've seen him."

She looked at me as if she really thought I might know. She has huge eyes, my mother, dark and soft as a cow's, and when she looks at you in this trusting and pleading way, not just hoping but *expecting* you to answer an absolutely impossible question, they can drive you mad. It's as if she had just given up. Handed everything over for someone else to look after. Had decided not to bother even to *think* for herself.

My father used to swear and throw things. I try not to act like my father.

I said, "I hope so. But I can't know, can I? I mean, I'm

[8]

amazingly brilliant in all sorts of ways, but I just don't happen to have second sight."

She smiled. A bit reproachful but still a smile. She said, "Oh, Plato, I don't know what I'd do without you."

"I wonder sometimes myself," I said.

◆

We got to Athens twenty minutes before the New York flight was due in. So of course she abandoned me in the baggage hall and sped off to meet it. By the time I had found a trolley, lugged her huge case off the carousel, and trundled along after her, she had disappeared in the howling mob that was surging around the passenger exit from Customs.

This scene was just typical of the difference between the Greeks and the English-Welsh I was talking about. At Heathrow Airport, in London, people waiting for friends and families might be a bit excited—peering, jumping up and down, waving. Even pushing and shoving a bit. But they don't carry on as if they were storming the Bastille. And if a policeman or a security guard tells them to stand back, they do what they're told. At once. Meekly.

Greeks don't have this respect for the law. Faced with the friends and relations of a full planeload of Greeks coming home from the New World, most sensible policemen would quickly find a more urgent job somewhere quieter. And in fact there wasn't a policeman in sight on this occasion, only a couple of red-faced security guards bobbing about in the crush, helpless as corks in the sea. When the first passengers began to appear, the guards disappeared. Trampled underfoot probably.

I was afraid for my mother. She is so small and light. I suddenly felt very indignant and English. There were lots of other little old ladies caught up in this crowd. Children, too. These roistering Greeks ought to be ashamed of themselves. Couldn't they see that if they just waited behind the barrier in a patient and orderly fashion no one would be hurt and the people they were meeting would be with them much quicker?

I stood on the trolley. I saw a woman with a baby in one arm and a suitcase in the other. She looked a bit scared and I was wondering if I should try to help her, take the baby or the suitcase, when she started laughing and crying together. An old man was struggling toward her, arms stretched out to her. She shouted, "Papa," and then they were clinging together, the baby between them, and the poor baby began to cry and the old man looked down at him and began to cry too. They were all crying, the little baby because he was frightened, but his mother and grandfather out of happiness at seeing each other.

I felt a bit tearful myself. "That's the Greek in you," I told myself sternly. Then I saw Aliki and jumped down from the trolley and pushed my way through to her, waving and yelling at the top of my voice like everyone else.

My mother got to her first. I had time to notice that she had to reach up to put her arms around Aliki, and to worry in case my little sister had grown taller than me, before I realized that she had come from New York alone.

My dad wasn't with her. Not even some way behind in the queue. Aliki and my mother were kissing and hugging and the other passengers swirled around them and past them, their faces either anxious and strained as they looked for their families or wild with joy as they saw them. And there was no sign of my father.

I wasn't sure whether I was pleased or sorry. Part of me had looked forward to seeing him and part of me had dreaded it so much it made me feel sick.

But there was a man with Aliki. Close behind her, anyway. A man who was looking at my mother and grinning away as if she were his long-lost sister. He was dark-haired and very Greek-looking, with that kind of straight line down the nose from the forehead that you see in old statues. He had a brilliant gold tooth in the front of his mouth. He said, "Maria."

Maria is my mother's name. I was beside her by then. I heard her catch her breath, as if in surprise. Then she gave a kind of groan and said, "*Tasso?*"

"No one else!" He held out his hands and she took them, laughing, but with a little break in her voice as if she might cry any moment.

I thought, *All this laughing and crying!* I said to Aliki, "They do carry on, these foreigners, don't they?"

She looked at me a bit blankly. I suppose it was too much to expect that we would be absolutely on the same wavelength when we hadn't seen each other for ages. So I changed tack and said, "You don't seem to have got any smaller. You aiming to get into the *Guinness Book of Records?* You and I are beginning to look like David and Goliath!"

I laughed to show I didn't mind being a midget. She said, "That's really *mean*, Plato." Her voice wobbled and tears came into her eyes—which are brown like our mother's, but very much paler, and neither so big nor so gentle. In fact, Aliki's eyes have quite a tigerish glint when she is upset or

angry. As she was now. She said—spat at me, rather—
"I'm not especially big for my age. It's just that American
children are naturally tall. I expect it's being better fed than
children in Europe."

Actually she said, "Yurrup." (Aliki sounds very American
nowadays, but I am going to ignore the phonetics and write
down what she says in ordinary English.)

"Aw, come off it, Al," I drawled, doing my best to copy
her accent. Then I remembered that she was only eleven and
that I really was pleased to see her. I said, "You look fine,
I'm just jealous, you know me. What's happened to Dad?"

"He couldn't come." For some reason she had gone pink.
She frowned and mouthed at me, "Tell you later."

All this time our mother and Tasso were jabbering away
to each other in Greek. I had tried to ignore them, not because
they were speaking their native language but because they
were standing with their arms wrapped around each other
gazing into each other's eyes like actors in a particularly
soppy film. I told myself this was perfectly *normal* for them.
In Greece people touch each other all the time. Even men
kiss each other when they meet, which is something you
would never see in England.

Tasso caught my eye. He didn't seem to mind being seen
snogging with my mother. Quite the opposite. He put his
arm round her shoulders and tucked her in close to him and
said, "I have met your charming sister on the plane. But
you and I have not met before. My name is Tasso
Psomodakis."

He held out his free hand and I took it. "Plato Jones," I
said. It suddenly seemed a rather plain sort of name.

Tasso said it was a pleasure to meet me. He held on to

my hand while he looked deeply into my eyes. He said, "Your mother and I went to school together. We have not met since."

"Just think, Plato," my mother said, with an excited giggle. "If Aliki and Tasso hadn't sat next to each other in the airplane we might never have met again ever."

I said, "And if your father wasn't dying you and I wouldn't have been here to meet them."

I meant that just as an interesting thought of a kind I could discuss with Uncle Emlyn: the importance of chance and luck in everyone's life—something like that. Uncle Emlyn may not talk much when his mother is around, but sometimes we go for long walks on the mountain and then there's no stopping him. Uncle Emlyn teaches math but he is a philosopher in his spare time. He says all human life is built around ideas; even scientific things like computers were discovered because people sat quietly alone and thought about basic principles.

But my mother is not interested in ideas. Only in feelings. She looked hurt, as if she thought I had meant that she had no business to laugh and be happy with her old friend at this sad time.

Tasso looked at me gravely and kindly. He said, "Good and bad can exist together, Plato. It is quite possible to grieve for a death and rejoice in a birth at the same time."

This was the sort of thing Uncle Emlyn might have said. Although Tasso didn't look in the least like him (Uncle Emlyn is a little man with a lot of wild white hair who always looks as if he has slept in his clothes), I thought they might be alike in other ways and it made me feel easier. Especially when he said, "I have my car waiting. It will be quicker than hiring a taxi. You will allow me to take you, won't you, Maria?"

My mother murmured something in Greek. She was looking up at him with her trusting cow eyes. He hugged her closer, as if to protect her, and said, "I think we should telephone before we leave. Aliki, you will wait here with Plato."

He spoke as if he assumed we would do exactly what he told us without any question. I looked at Aliki, expecting her to explode. Or at least to look sulky. She hates being ordered about. But she was gazing at Tasso with an adoring expression.

"He's got a big new Mercedes," she said as soon as he was out of earshot. "He told me on the plane. It's got white leather seats. And he's wearing a *gigantic* gold ring, did you see? He must be just fabulously rich."

She rolled her eyes upward as if she were watching Tasso Psomodakis ascending to heaven on a fluffy white cloud.

I said, "It is easier for a camel to go through the eye of a needle than for a rich man to enter into the kingdom of God."

(The reason I am so quick on the draw with the correct quote from the Bible is that when I was younger my Welsh grandmother used to send me a text to learn every week, and when I went to visit her she gave me a pound for each one I remembered.)

"I don't care about going to heaven. I love money more than anything," Aliki said.

CHAPTER·2

I might have quarreled with Aliki then. She is so digustingly *greedy*. That's why she wanted to live with our father instead of our mother; she thought she would have a better time, more clothes and toys and things like her own television and stereo. And more money.

Dad married this dentist called Barbie (her real name is Barbara, but Barbie is what I call her for obvious reasons). Dentists in the United States are seriously rich. Americans spend more money on their teeth than people in other countries spend on feeding their families. My father, who works for a computer company, doesn't do badly either, even though he has to send a monthly check to Mum and me.

Aliki is happy with our father and Barbie-the-Dentist-Doll, but she misses our mother too, and that's something she doesn't know how to handle. She gets angry the moment she sees us. I don't know why. Maybe she just hates to think we have been getting by all right without her. Picking a good fight with me makes her feel better.

But it didn't work this time. Our mother came back at the critical moment (while I was still thinking of something really nasty to say to Aliki and Aliki was waiting steely-eyed and red-faced for me to say it) to tell us our grandfather was dead. He had died half an hour ago.

Mum wasn't crying. She said, "Now, darlings, you mustn't be too upset. He was a very old man."

Aliki and I looked at each other. We often went to Greece to stay with our mother's Aunt Elena, but Nikos Petropoulos, our grandfather, lived alone in his village in the mountains, and we had only seen him once or twice—years ago, when we were both too small to remember.

I could see that Aliki wanted to say no one could be really upset when a person died whom she hardly knew, but she stopped herself. Not for our mother's sake, but because she was so keen to make a good impression on Tasso.

He was making himself useful, checking we had all our baggage, getting a porter, even reminding Mum to make sure she had put the return tickets safely away in her purse. As if he knew as well as I did that she was likely to lose them. As if it was *his* job to look after her. I wondered if I minded him taking charge, taking over, and decided I didn't. It made a nice change.

I had only been to Greece in the summer before, and although I knew it was winter now, I was still surprised to find the wind was freezing when we got outside the building. Aliki put on a great act of moaning and shivering—*Oh, poor little, cold little me*—and Mum laughed, and hugged her, and turned up the collar of her pink, padded jacket.

[16]

"It will be warm in the car, Princess," Tasso said, winking at me to show he had got my young sister's measure. I pretended not to notice the wink. I thought he was altogether too pleased with himself.

I wondered why we were hanging about in the cold. I should have known Tasso was too grand to fetch his Mercedes from the car park himself. It drew up in front of us with a hiss and a whisper. The driver got out and he and Tasso hugged and kissed and thumped each other the way Greek men do. They jabbered away in Foreign for a while and then Tasso handed Mum into the passenger seat and the driver turned to Aliki and me. He said, "Welcome," grinning away behind an enormous, wiry moustache, and I thought, for a horrible moment, he was going to kiss me. But he just patted my shoulder and pinched Aliki's cheek and then opened the back door of the car.

The inside gleamed white and gold. Mercifully, the leather seat in back was covered with plastic, otherwise we would have needed a bath before we dared sit on it. Even Aliki was awed. She poked me in the ribs and giggled.

Tasso got into the driver's seat and started the engine. Millions of lights flashed in front of him—enough for a spaceship. He spoke to the driver through the open window and they both shouted with laughter.

Mum turned around. "All right, my darlings?" she said. "Aren't we lucky to have met Tasso?"

I knew what she meant. Tasso was someone she could trust to look after her. But I had been doing my best.

I said, "We could have got a taxi quite easily."

◆

I am not going to describe the drive to Iria because descriptions are boring. And it was dark, anyway, so there was nothing to see. The only thing I want to mention is that after we had left Athens we were in the mountains. And the curious thing about mountains is that you can feel them around you even when you can't see them. There is a kind of thick silence. Like fog. Pressure on the eardrums because of the altitude, Uncle Emlyn would say. But it feels more mysterious.

Tasso talked to us to begin with. Various adult stupidities like, "Plato, you must learn to speak Greek. Your mother says you are clever." But Aliki fell asleep almost at once and I pretended I hadn't heard him. So he gave up trying to ingratiate himself and put a tape on. It was nothing I knew. Some kind of sweet, throbbing music, not loud, but loud enough to make it hard to hear what he said to my mother.

They were speaking Greek, anyway. It was a long time since I had heard her talk Foreign and it made her seem different. A different person. Her voice went up and down more, quick and excited. She laughed rather more than seemed right, somehow. Since she was going to bury her father, I mean. I knew he would be buried because cremation is illegal in Greece.

Then I thought, there was no reason why she shouldn't laugh if she felt like it. Even if she was sorry about her father she might not feel like crying the whole time. She had been born in the mountain village but her mother had died soon after she was born, and Aunt Elena, who was her mother's younger sister, had taken the baby home with her and brought her up in the family house in Iria. My mother had never lived in the village; she had never spent even a night with her father.

"I used to think he didn't want me," she once told Aliki and me. "Now I don't think it was that, more that he thought I was better off with Aunt Elena. But you don't know how lucky you are, having a proper dad around as well as a mummy!"

That was before my father walked out, of course. *He* said that Nikos Petropulos was the kind of man who "liked his own company." He looked after his olives and his goats and his bees and liked to be alone to read in the evenings. "I thought he was a good man," my father had said—speaking rather sternly, as if other people had said that he wasn't.

I wondered why Dad hadn't come. But Aliki was asleep on my shoulder.

It was more than three hours to Iria and after a while I went to sleep too. I must have slept deeply because when I woke there was an old woman sitting beside me. Almost *on* me, in fact. She wore dusty- and fusty-smelling black clothes, and as the Mercedes swept around bends she crossed herself and cackled with fear. In between she rattled away like machine-gun fire to my mother and Tasso.

She paid no attention to me. I was just a convenient cushion to her. When Tasso stopped the car to let her out, she made use of me to heave herself up, bony hand crushing my thighbone, and didn't once glance in my direction. Not even when she stood on my foot. I thought she must have been terrified out of her wits by Tasso's driving.

But she wasn't frightened. She stood on the side of the road, lit from below by the lights of the car, looking wild and witchlike. I could see the black hair in her nostrils, and her brown, crooked teeth, and the dry white underneath of her tongue as she shouted and shook her fists at us.

My mother said, "I won't *listen*. Please, Tasso . . ."

The car leapt forward at once, swerving round the old woman, who thumped on the roof as it passed. A scatter of stones hit the back window and Tasso swore. That is, I assume he was swearing. I thought, *That could be a real reason for learning Greek. I could swear in front of my Welsh grandmother!*

Aliki woke and started grumbling and groaning. I said, "What was all that hullabaloo?"

Aliki said, "What hullabaloo?"

"Nothing, Princess," Tasso said. "No problem. Nothing to disturb your sweet dreams. We gave a lift to an old lady who was afraid to be in the car."

"She sounded angry," I said.

"She comes from Molo," our mother said. "From my father's village."

She sounded strange. Quite calm, but a forced calm, as if underneath she was boiling.

Tasso said, "Forget her, Maria. She is one of the mad ones."

I said, "What was she angry about?"

Tasso said, "She was arguing, Plato. It was a matter of politics. An old story. Greeks live with their history. Fifty years ago is like yesterday to them, and they bear very long grudges. Old scores take a long time to settle."

My mother said, "Don't ask too many questions, Plato darling."

Aliki started whining. "I'm hungry!"

Aliki is always hungry when she can't think of anything else to do. I said, "If we've got as far as the village already, then it won't be much longer. Not much farther to Iria."

◆

Not much farther by car and on a good paved road. But when CLJ had escaped from his cave above the village of Molo, it had taken him two and a half days, following goat tracks over the mountains and only moving at night because of the Germans. Elena, his guide, was fifteen years old; she had been sent by her parents to live with friends in the village because although it was occupied by the enemy it was less dangerous than the town. And, at that time of the war, the people in Greek towns were starving.

Elena took CLJ to her parents' house in Iria, and they hid him and shared what scraps of food they could find with him until the message came that the submarine was waiting out in the bay.

During the war, most of the people in Iria hid English and American soldiers and airmen who were on the run from the Germans. It was especially dangerous to hide CLJ, who was a spy. Two of the German soldiers in Iria were billeted in Elena's house, and as CLJ lay hidden under the floorboards of the storeroom on the ground floor he could hear them tramping above him, up and down the stairs, shouting to one another and laughing. But at night, when they were asleep, Aunt Elena always came to let him out and gave him water to wash in, and something to eat, and the latest newspaper. While CLJ ate and read and stretched himself, she stood guard at the door of the storeroom, listening for sounds from the street and from the room on the floor above where the German soldiers were sleeping.

Aliki thinks it's a pity that CLJ was already married to our Welsh grandmother when Aunt Elena rescued him because it would have been romantic if he could have married her. But I don't think Aunt Elena could ever have been the sort of silly girl who thought all that much about love and getting married. Aliki is going to be that kind of girl if someone doesn't watch out for her. She doesn't think about anything except boys and clothes and what she looks like. She's always looking at herself—in mirrors, shop windows, any bit of glass, however dim and murky.

Aunt Elena is old now, but I don't think she would have looked in mirrors very often even when she was young. She is tall and thin and fierce-looking, and her face is crisscrossed with deep lines that look as if they were drawn with a sharp mapping pen. She isn't the sort of woman you could ever think of calling by her first name. Even her friends in Iria call her Kyria Elena. *Kyria* is one of the few Greek words I know. It sounds better than *Mrs.*

◆

We were in the plain and we could see Iria ahead of us: the great rock black against the sky, with the huge castle cascading down the side of it, the battlements silvery in the moonlight, and the lights of the town twinkling below it. It seemed welcoming from a distance, but as the big Mercedes crawled through the narrow streets, it was like a dead town. There were one or two people about, hurrying along close to the walls of the houses, heads bent against the wind, but there were no strolling families, no busy tables outside the tavernas, no old men selling chestnuts at the street corners, no children playing, no Gypsies begging. No tourists. No music. No laughter. Well, of course, it was winter.

I said, "It's like the *Marie Celeste.*" For my ignorant sister's benefit, I added, "That was a ship, found drifting with no crew on board but everything just as if they had left five minutes earlier, food on the table, still warm . . ."

Aliki groaned. "I don't *need* this. Why do you always want to *tell* me things, Plato! I don't need to *know!*" She put her hands over her ears.

"Have you not been here in winter before?" Tasso grinned at me over his shoulder. "In winter, it is all indoors. Like in England. Everyone shut away in their own private houses. Keeping themselves to themselves. That's what you say, isn't it?"

Aunt Elena's house is in a tiny square. It is a big, ancient house built on the side of the hill with marble steps leading up to the door. It would be quite a grand house if it were not so tumbledown. There are creaky wooden shutters; little, rickety iron balconies that look as if they might fall off any minute; an old marble lion with only one ear; and a tiny garden full of lemon trees and lilies and geraniums in pots. The front door is usually open when we come, and Aunt Elena is waiting.

Not this time. The house was dark. The shutters were closed. And the moment we got out of the car, the priest's fat wife from the house opposite, next to the church, came flying out, black clothes billowing, screeching at the top of her voice. "Kyria Elena" was all I understood. She went flapping up the marble steps like an overweight blackbird.

[23]

There was a rattle of keys, the door was opened, the light switched on.

"Aunt Elena's not here," Aliki said. She sounded as if she really thought she was telling us something.

"Of course not," my mother said. "She's up in the village with Papa."

She spoke as if this was something we should have known without being told. She and Aliki have quite a lot in common.

"Why?" Aliki drawled out this question in a rude, sing-song way. As if she knew for certain that there was no possible answer.

If I had been our mother, I would have slapped her. But Mum said, gently and patiently, "She couldn't leave my papa alone, my darling."

Mum laughed and then, as if that was the end of the matter, ran up the marble steps to wave her hands about and chatter away to the priest's wife. Tasso followed her, hung about with her baggage like a porter.

So, as usual, it was left to me to do the explaining. I said, "When someone dies in Greece, they don't pack them off straightaway to the undertaker's. They keep the corpse in the house and sit with it till it's buried. They never leave it alone for a minute. All the friends and relations come to visit and say goodbye. And they light lamps and candles so the dead person's soul will have light."

Mum had told me this on the plane. I thought it was sweet and sad. But Aliki was pulling a disgusted face. I thought I'd give her something to be disgusted about. I said, "He'll be buried tomorrow. It's the custom in Greece. I suppose he might start to stink otherwise. But before he's put in a coffin we'll be taken to see him. Mum says we'll probably be expected to kiss him."

She gaped at me, mouth open, eyes wide.

I said, "And there's another thing. When you've been buried about five years, they dig you up. They collect all the bones. They try to pick up the skull first, then the rib bones, then all the other bits. And if the bones are clean and white, that means all your sins have left you, so they wash them in wine and put them in a box."

"Ugh," Aliki said faintly. "That's really *gross.*"

She looked a greenish color and I began to feel I'd been mean. I said, "Just different, that's all. Different from home."

I wondered where home was for her now. Before our father went to New York he had been working in London and we had all lived together in the suburb where Mum and I were living now. But although England was still home for me, Aliki was partly American as well as partly British and partly Greek. She was more mixed up than I was.

She was shivering. She said, "I'd rather die than kiss a dead person."

"At least he can't bite you," I said, growling and snapping my jaws at her to make her laugh.

But instead she started to cry like a baby and I was sorry. I gave her a hug and said, "It'll be all right. I'll see you don't have to go close to him—you can get behind me and no one will notice."

She went all soft and droopy then, and I realized from the way she had to sag at the knees to put her head on my shoulder that the worst thing of all had finally happened.

❂ CHAPTER·3

My kid sister was taller than I was.

This humiliating discovery occupied my mind all through my grandfather's funeral. I tried not to stand too close to Aliki so that no one else should notice my shame. I hadn't forgotten my promise to shield her from the horrid sight of her grandfather's dead body, but by the time she was actually faced with it, she was enjoying herself too much to need my protection. Wild horses would have been needed to drag her away from his coffin.

From the moment she got up that morning there had been no more sensitive moaning about not kissing dead people. She moaned *once*—when she heard that Tasso was not coming with us. But after that she hardly said anything except to point out that the taxi that took us up to the village wasn't as comfortable as his Mercedes. She sat very quiet, holding a small bunch of frostbitten roses that Mum had found somewhere and looking soulful. From time to time she puffed out a little sigh, as if to remind us that this was a very sad day in her life, and I knew she was actually having a whale of a time. I think Mum realized it too; she caught my eye and smiled.

There is only one road to the village of Molo. It comes to an end in a little square with a church and a big plane tree, and the houses straggle above and below it. We left the taxi in the square and walked around the church and along a mud path. Aliki stopped once to look at the white nanny goat that bleated and ran the length of its chain when it saw us; otherwise she continued to act the part of Chief Mourner, clutching the roses against her and sighing. Mum had stopped watching her, though. She was looking nervously from side to side of the path—almost as if she were expecting someone to jump out at us and say *boo!*

It seemed a bit strange, but I didn't really think about it, just registered the fact in my mental computer without wondering what it might mean. As I said, I was bugged, haunted, obsessed, and *tormented* by the extra half inch or so by which my little sister now overtopped me. Although my best friend, Jane Tucker (who comes into this story later), is taller than I am, I can just about bear it because Jane is older. But Aliki-the-Giantess is two and a half years younger than I am.

My grandfather's house is on the edge of the village. (Mum and I had gone to see him the last time we came to Iria on holiday but he hadn't been there. Aunt Elena said Nikos must have gone to see if his olives were ready for harvest, but I remember thinking that was odd, since he must have known we were coming.) We met no one on the path now, and if I hadn't been distracted by my failure to grow, I would have known that was odd too; the village is usually a bustling and lively place, people passing, calling out to each other.

Though of course it was winter, and chilly.

The house is below the path: a small stone house with a terrace outside, and a vine, and a woodpile, and a rough sort of garden that tumbles away down the mountain. There was still no one about. I heard my mother mutter something to herself. It sounded like, "I wonder what they've done with the cats." Then she lifted her chin as if she had suddenly decided to face up to something and started down the steps to the house.

Aunt Elena came to the open front door. She was all in black with a black scarf on her head. She held my mother in her arms and looked beyond her at Aliki and me. She said, "Why have you brought the children, Maria?"

She shook her head and frowned, as if she had not meant to say this in front of us, and came quickly to kiss us. She said, "Welcome, Plato. Welcome, Aliki." Her moustache was sharp as needles but Aliki didn't jerk away or pull a face; she endured the prickly kiss with a martyred and dreamy expression. She said in a soft, breathy voice, "I am so sorry your brother-in-law is dead, Aunt Elena."

I thought it was quite clever of Aliki to have worked out this relationship. I knew that Elena was our mother's aunt, and that our dead grandmother had been Elena's sister, but I hadn't bothered to think any further. Greeks are keen on families. I thought, *Perhaps Aliki has a lot of Greek in her.*

Aunt Elena looked from Aliki to me and back again. As if *measuring* us. I felt dizzy with shame. Then she put her arm around Aliki's shoulders and walked her to the house.

My mother said to me, "I couldn't bear to come on my own. I'm sorry I'm such a coward, Plato."

I didn't know what she meant. At that moment I didn't care particularly either. I smiled in what I hoped was a reassuring way and said, "Cheer up, it can't be any worse than going to the dentist." (It isn't just the existence of Barbie-the-Dentist-Doll that makes me equate dentists with devilish practices; between twelve and thirteen I had a distinctly squalid experience with braces on my teeth.)

Mum looked surprised for a minute, then decided not to waste time wondering what I was talking about. She smiled and tucked my hand through her arm. She murmured, "I hope Aliki won't be too upset."

Why *Aliki*? Why not *me*? Why is it only girls who are expected to have delicate feelings?

"Aliki upset? Fat chance," I snarled. "Old Rhinoceros Hide!"

Though I had to admit, a few minutes later, observing Aliki's performance as a grief-stricken granddaughter, that only another put-upon older brother would be likely to agree with me.

◆

It was darker inside the house than outside. The only light came from a thick white candle stuck between my grandfather's hands, which were folded across his chest, and from two red-shaded lamps at the head of his coffin. A white sheet covered his bottom half, and his top half was dressed in a jacket and a shirt and a tie. There was an icon, a colored picture of a saint, propped up on his legs.

My eyes got used to the gloom. Women in black stood round the coffin, crowded together; I could see the whites of their eyes gleam in the shadows. My grandfather's face was better lit, by the candles and the lamps, and although he looked *dead* all right, his eyes closed and a cloth tied under his chin to stop his jaw falling open, he didn't look as frightening as I had imagined. Just still and smoothed out and peaceful and somehow empty—like a husk, or a nutshell.

I don't know if Aliki had been scared when she first saw him. Even if she had been, she wasn't scared now. She was standing by the head of the coffin and looking down at the poor old corpse with the kind of soppy-sad look on her face that would make any reasonable person want to throw up. If she could have squeezed out a tear it would have been more repulsive, but even Aliki-the-Tragedy-Queen couldn't quite manage that.

Instead, when she looked up and saw everyone watching her, she stepped forward, head bowed as if she were praying, and put her winter roses on our grandfather's chest. Then she waited, looking up again and around her in a suddenly timid way at all those shadowy, white-eyed women, as if she wasn't sure what to do next, and all at once I was on her side and quite sorry for her. Although she had been pretending, it was only in the way people pretend when they are trying to do what they think they ought to do. Or what other people seem to expect them to do. And Aliki hadn't had much practice at funerals.

Nor had I, for that matter. I wondered if my mother was going to do something really embarrassing—like throwing herself on her papa's dead body and wailing. I was relieved when she said, in a perfectly normal voice, "I have brought my children so they can say farewell to Nikos Petropoulos."

I wondered why she should bother to say something so obvious, and say it in *English*. After all, Aliki and I knew why we were here! But then she was speaking in Greek, and the women were answering her, all of them rattling away like machine guns, and some of them coming forward to shake hands and kiss her, leaning over the coffin or pushing around it, and I saw Aliki go red with shame. Now everyone else was carrying on in this noisy way, she felt she had made a silly mistake in behaving so quietly and solemnly. I wondered if she was afraid all these women were talking about her. Though it sounded to me more as if they were quarreling with our mother, in spite of the handshakes and kisses.

I pulled a face at Aliki, screwing up my nose and waggling my ears to make her laugh, but her lower lip had started to tremble.

Aunt Elena said, "Plato, take Aliki outside. The priest will be coming soon and we will be going to the church. You should be out in the air while you can."

This was an order. Aunt Elena was not the sort of person to make a gentle suggestion to anyone. Aliki looked startled, and I guessed it was a long time since anyone had told her what to do in quite that tone of voice. I said, "Come on, Al," coaxing her, because there was something in Aunt Elena's expression that made me uneasy.

Aliki said, when we were outside on the terrace, "She didn't want us to hear what they were saying to Mum."

The same thought had struck me. Though it didn't seem likely. I said, "We couldn't understand them. She knows that."

"I know a bit of Greek. More than you, anyway," Aliki said smugly.

"What were they saying, then? Go on, you tell me!'

"I hate you," Aliki said. "Plato Constantine Jones, sometimes I really do hate you."

"I can't see why. It was you said you understood Greek, wasn't it?"

"Not that sort of Greek. Not that kind of real *talking* Greek. They say things too fast."

Someone said, "Ba-ba-ba-ba." And laughed.

A boy was standing on the path above the house. When we turned to look up at him he laughed again, in an excited, jeering way, and ran off up the path calling to someone else, someone I couldn't see, who shouted in answer.

"Behind that house, up there, *hiding*," Aliki said.

I looked where she pointed but saw no one. Apart from the women in the house, that boy was the only person I had seen since we came to the village. I had the feeling, suddenly, that they were all there, all the villagers, but hiding from us. Hiding—and watching. Eyes everywhere. It was a spooky sensation.

As if she felt it too, Aliki moved closer to me. She whispered, "What did he mean? Ba-ba-ba-ba?"

"Barbarians. It's what the Greeks call people who don't speak their language. What we say sounds just like ba-ba-ba to them. That's where the word comes from."

She said in a shocked voice, "I'm an American girl. Not a barbarian."

"You're a barbarian to them."

The church bell began to toll, the solemn sound rolling on the still air. Aliki said, "Is that for *him?*"

[32]

I thought she was looking fearful. I said, "I expect so. I expect it means that the priest will come soon and they'll take him to the church and after that to the graveyard. You'll have to go to the church, but if you don't want to watch him being buried I'm sure you don't have to. You could wait in the square till it's over, I'm sure that'll be all right. I can stay with you."

She said scornfully, "That'll be the best bit, putting the body down into the grave and pouring wine over it. That's what Dad said they'd do. What I don't like is this *place*. Everyone hiding and angry. Why don't they like us?"

I said, "Why should you think they don't?"

But I knew why. Though it wasn't a matter of thinking, it was a matter of feeling. You could feel it around you, pressing in on you. No one wanted us here. I thought perhaps it was just the winter; the village that was so bright and full of flowers in the summer seemed a mean, muddy place in the cold, sunless light. People weren't hiding from us. They were indoors, keeping warm!

Then I saw the boy again and knew this wasn't true.

He wasn't alone this time. There were five of them altogether, almost-grown-up bully-boys, knobby arms and legs sticking out of their clothes, straggling along the path, horsing about, shoving at each other, and pretending to be freaked out with laughter whenever they looked in our direction.

I said to Aliki, "I wonder why they find us so risible." I thought if I used a word she didn't know she would be too angry with me to be frightened.

But then one of them picked up a stone. It was only a little stone and he threw it without much force, so that it

[33]

trickled rather than bounced across the terrace. But it was meant as a threat.

I said, "Perhaps we'd better go in the house."

Aliki shook her head. She took a couple of steps forward and shouted, "Get away, stupid boys. If you've got nothing better to do, why don't you just clear off home and get your mothers to put you to bed."

That made them laugh louder, of course. Aliki bent and picked up the stone and threw it back. It hit one of the boys on his ankle. He yelped and hopped, clutching his injured foot, and the others fell silent. Their silence, and the absolute stillness that went along with it, was suddenly menacing.

Aliki felt it. She got behind me. As if she hadn't noticed yet that I wasn't tall enough to hide her. She said, "Oh, Plato," and giggled.

I said, "Barbarian. Half-witted barbarian. You only throw stones at people bigger than you if your name is David and you're quite sure you've got God on your side."

"They won't hurt us. Aunt Elena wouldn't let them."

Although she sounded bold enough, she didn't budge from behind me. I thought I had better take off my glasses. I knew from painful experience that if it came to a fight I would be bashed up if I kept them on, so I might as well be bashed up without them. It was more economical.

I said, "I don't know that Aunt Elena could stop them. You'd better take care of these for me." I folded my goggles and handed them to Aliki.

The world misted over. Looking up at the path I could see ghostly figures moving about, backward and forward, in a sort of shimmering dance. Then one of them, the tallest and broadest phantom, seemed to detach itself and come closer, advancing down the steps to the terrace.

I told myself it was better not to be able to see the fist that was going to hit me. Though this is an argument that I have never found altogether convincing.

Aliki said, "It's all right. They're running awy."

It was the first time that taking my glasses off had had that effect. I peered into the fog. I couldn't see anything. I said, "Am I so frightening?"

"Silly," she said. "It was the *priest*. The priest coming."

◆

By the time I had my glasses back on the priest had passed by and gone into the house and the boys had disappeared altogether. And from then on, for quite a while, nothing out of the ordinary happened. Unless you count a Greek village funeral as being something out of the ordinary, which it was for my sister and me, of course, but not for anyone else who was there.

Aliki and I waited on the terrace until they all came out of the house. Two men carried the coffin up the steps to the path, where they put it on a little cart. All we could see of it was the mound of flowers that covered the body. The priest was a huge man, wearing a gold and purple cape and a high black hat that that made him look even taller. He stood to one side, his folded hands resting comfortably on the shelf of his stomach, while one of the women fetched a donkey and backed it into the shafts and buckled the harness, and another woman stood at the donkey's head and led it up the path to the church. All the women were in black, with black scarves on their heads, and although my mother was wearing black too, her new coat had gold buttons and a pretty fur collar, and it made her look quite different from the others—younger and richer and smarter.

When we got to the square, the men lifted the coffin off the cart and carried it into the church, which was lit by thick white candles like the one between my grandfather's hands. My mother and Aunt Elena stood at the head of the coffin and Aliki and I stood behind them. The priest sang the service, which seemed to me to go on forever; all I could think of was how long I could manage to balance myself on the balls of my feet so that to people behind me I would look at least the same height as Aliki.

All the muscles at the backs of my legs were burning by the time we got to the kissing of the corpse, which took me by surprise even though I knew it was going to happen. Aliki hissed at me, "Do I have to?" But before I could answer she was bending over the coffin. Her long hair fell forward so I couldn't tell whether she had actually kissed him or not. Then it was my turn. I had never seen a dead person before, let alone touched one, and I suddenly began to feel distinctly peculiar. I was afraid I might freak out and gibber. But it wasn't so bad; Nikos Petropoulos's forehead was cold and dry and the only smell was of flowers.

It wasn't until we came out of the church that the really frightening thing happened. The square had been empty when we went in but it was now crowded with stiff, silent people, standing and staring. No one moved or spoke as the coffin was carried out and put on the donkey cart, but as we fell in behind and the funeral procession began to move from the square, I saw a man who had stepped aside to let us pass turn and spit against the Evil Eye. It was so quiet I could hear his spit hiss on the ground. Aunt Elena put her arm round my mother.

Aliki said, "I expect they're saying goodbye to him. That's what Dad said might happen. After someone dies, friends go to the house to pay their respects. I suppose the house is too small for everyone to squash in, so they're paying their respects in the square."

It had seemed to me that the way we were being watched (let alone spat at) was hardly friendly, and the sooner we were out of the village the better. But I didn't say so to Aliki. Other people might think she was older than I was because she was taller, but I knew that Aliki-the-Bean-Pole was only a little girl of eleven.

Not that there was any need to look out for her, really. Some girls have delicate feelings, but there is nothing delicate about my young sister.

The funeral procession straggled along the road from the square and then turned off down a steep, muddy path. The donkey cart lurched in the ruts and the coffin slithered from side to side. The graveyard was some way down the mountain, a very small oblong of land surrounded by a dry-stone wall and overgrown with tall grasses.

It was a dreary and desolate place. There were a few graves that had marble headstones and were decorated with dried flowers and colored stones and framed photographs, but most of them were abandoned—just pits, with the dry earth fallen in and rickety wooden fences around them.

Aliki whispered, "D'you know what? I expect those graves

are empty because the skeleton of the last person has been dug up and they don't bother to fill them in so it'll be less trouble when they come to bury the next one."

This seemed a ghoulish thought to me, but Aliki was pink with excitement. "I wonder where they put the *bones*," she said thoughtfully. "Would they fit into a shoe box? I mean, you could take them home and keep them in the house, on top of the wardrobe or under the bed."

I was beginning to feel distinctly queasy. "I suppose some people might do that." I wondered why they would want to. I said, "If they were very fond of the person. But there's usually a special place in the graveyard."

"I know," Aliki said importantly. "Dad told me. It's called an ossuary."

This was rather a grand word for the brick lean-to in the corner of the graveyard where tin boxes were stacked, some of them neatly labeled with the names and photographs of the people whose remains were inside. Other boxes spilled out their contents on the dirt floor. Aliki touched a small gray skull with her toe. "Yuck," she said. "Gross."

But her eyes shone like lamps. As Uncle Emlyn says, women are really contrary! Aliki had been so squeamish when I had told her about digging up the dead bodies, but now she was actually faced with her first *human head*, she was cool as a breeze.

I was the one who felt sick. I said, "You're supposed to be attending your grandfather's burial, not gloating over some stranger's old bones."

I was angrier with myself than with her. It was disgustingly feeble to start quaking and shivering at this harmless evidence of mortality. I thought, *We will all be bones one day. Even Aliki.*

She didn't seem worried. She said, "We'll miss the best bit if we don't hurry."

I didn't know if she meant the pouring of the wine and oil over the body or the closing of the coffin. Mum had said that sometimes close relations, widows, or a son or a daughter, would throw themselves into the grave, screaming and sobbing. She had been trying to warn me so I wouldn't be shocked if something like that were to happen. But I was shocked just to think of it. My mouth had gone dry and my head was buzzing.

I followed Aliki. She pushed her way through the women standing at the graveside to get a better view. I couldn't see anything. Then a woman said very loudly, in English, "May God forgive him."

It was my mother. Someone moved aside in front of me and I could see her. She was standing at the edge of the grave. She looked up and saw me. She looked sad but quite calm. She gave me a little smile and I thought she was telling me not to be frightened. I tried to smile back but my face had gone stiff and the buzzing in my head had grown louder and a dark pit seemed to open in front of me. And I felt myself falling.

CHAPTER · 4

As I got into the taxi, Aliki said in a hushed voice, "You would have fallen into the grave if Aunt Elena hadn't been there to catch you."

She sounded as if she thought I had done something wonderful instead of just making a fool of myself.

Luckily for my self-respect, I didn't remember too much. They must have loaded me onto the donkey cart while I was unconscious. I had woken up to find myself slithering about on the floor of the cart with the wheels squeaking and grinding beneath me and decided to keep my eyes closed. Better to be dead, or at least in a coma, than to face the embarrassment of my position! Then I started to wonder about my glasses. I couldn't feel them on my nose. Suppose they had fallen into the grave and the earth had been shoveled on top of them? I put up my hand and Mum said, close to my ear, "It's all right, they're safe in my handbag."

I have to admit that my mother can be quite sensible in

an emergency. She didn't make a fuss, not even later on in the taxi, just got into the passenger seat next to the driver and chattered away to him in staccato Greek without once turning round to check on her poor, frail invalid son!

To be honest, at this point I couldn't help feeling that she was being a little *too* sensible. Just a mite *casual*, in fact. After all I might have fainted again, and if you faint *sitting up*, the blood drains from your brain and you can end up quite gaga. Batty. Totally and terminally moronic.

Then I thought, *Perhaps she's ashamed of me, passing out like that in front of all her father's old friends.*

Except that they hadn't seemed to be friends. Certainly not all those silent watchers in the square.

I began to feel sick and shuddery again. Something had felt so horribly wrong in that village! I said, "Mum, why did you say, 'God forgive him'? I mean, what had your father *done?*"

She turned round and looked at me, frowning. "What do you mean, Plato? 'May God forgive him' is just what you say at a Greek burial. At the graveside. It's part of the service, like the priest saying in the church, 'Let us give a farewell kiss to him whom death has taken.' That's all, darling. Really."

I knew by the way she gave a funny half-laugh that there was something more but that she wasn't planning to tell me. My mother isn't exactly a *secretive* person; she just has this fixed idea in her mind that there are some things "children" wouldn't understand and so shouldn't be told. Where my mother is concerned you have to be a good detective to find out what is going on. A kind of spy, really.

In the beginning, when Dad first left us, and later, when

he married Barbie-the-Dentist-Doll, I became a dab hand at steaming letters open and listening to telephone calls on the extension. I needed to find out what was going to happen to Aliki and me, and necessity is the mother of invention, as Uncle Emlyn would say. And perhaps the genes I have inherited from CLJ helped a little. I rather think of myself as Jones-the-Spy-Junior.

Though of course only a quarter of me comes from CLJ. Another quarter from my Welsh grandmother—who is not an ancestor I am keen to resemble. My Greek grandmother I never knew. And my Greek grandfather does not appear to have been exactly mourned by his village!

I gave my mother one more chance. I said, "You know what I mean, Mum. The way they were all going on. Why Aunt Elena thought you shouldn't have taken us to the funeral."

She looked at me reproachfully and her huge eyes slowly dampened with tears. My mother can turn on the tap whenever it suits her, so I wasn't too impressed. I said, "We would have had to be blind and deaf not to notice."

She shook her head as if in wonder that her only son could be so cruel to her. "Oh, Plato," she said, with a catch in her voice. "How can you be so unkind to me when I have just buried my poor papa?"

Her lower lip was trembling and the tears were gathering now, ready to fall. I was beginning to feel guilty when Aliki came to my rescue. "Those big boys were horrid. They laughed at us but they were really angry."

Our mother sighed. "There are a lot of stupid people in that village. They quarreled with my papa—oh, such a long time ago, but some of them still hold it against him. I don't want to think about it, let alone talk about it. What is there to talk about, after all? Nothing actually *happened* today. Just a few people with nothing better to do standing about and looking bored and bad-tempered."

She gave one of her half-laughs. Her eyes were dry now. She had talked herself out of her sadness—if, indeed, she had been sad in the first place. She said, "You have too much imagination, Plato darling."

She looked at me innocently, smiling, and I knew there was no point in asking more questions. If my mother doesn't care to think about something, then she can easily persuade herself that it never happened. And it's a short step from that to making you wonder if you have made it all up for some curious reason. Or dreamed it. Not this time, though. Not me. I was certain there was a mystery about my Greek grandfather and I was determined to solve it.

◆

A less important mystery was cleared up more easily. When we got back to Iria, the big Mercedes was waiting in the little square, and Mum packed us off to have an ice cream while she "made a few telephone calls" (Grown-up-Speak for having a quiet drink with Childhood Friend without the kids listening).

"Barbie's having a baby, that's why Dad couldn't come," Aliki said—or, rather, whispered, leaning across the café table beside the steamed-up window. "She didn't want him to leave her alone and she made him stay. It was really *gross*, the way she kept moaning."

There was no need to whisper. In the summer this was the best place in Iria for ices, but on this cold day we were the only customers and the waiter spoke no English. Even if he had done, he could hardly have heard anything either of us said. He was sitting with his feet up on another table and his whole attention fixed on the television that was blaring away on the counter.

I said, "I thought you liked Barbie."

She wriggled her shoulders. I could see what had happened. I said, "You think she won't bother with you when she's got her own baby?" Then I thought of something that was going to make much more trouble much sooner. "Does Mum know?"

Aliki shook her head. She looked miserable. "Dad said I wasn't to tell her. He said he'd write a letter for me to take, but he didn't."

I snorted. "Typical!"

The flood came up in her cheeks. "There wasn't much time. Don't be mean." But she sounded halfhearted.

"Okay," I said. "*Okay*. You stick up for him if you want to. Make excuses."

"I expect it's *her* fault," Aliki said. "I expect she made him. She's like that."

I didn't know what she meant and I wasn't sure I wanted to know. There were other things more important. Chiefly how my mother would feel. But there was the money, too. Although Mum had a job in the estate agent's office on the ground floor of our building, it was only part time, and without Dad's check we would have been skint at the end of the month. If the Dentist-Doll gave up work to have a baby, or if she had to pay someone to look after it, my father might not be so keen to support his old, cast-off family as well as his nice, shiny, new one. And the estate agency hadn't been doing well lately. My mother said the manager only kept her on because she was pretty.

Aliki said, "I expect I'll come back and live with you in England."

She sounded astonished, as if she had only just thought of this possibility. It seemed to perk her up wonderfully. She grinned at me, her mouth painted with ice cream, like a clown's.

"We can't afford you," I said. "Girls like you cost a lot. And you wouldn't like it. You're an American now—you keep saying so."

She pouted her clown's mouth at me. "I'm all the other things inside, just like you are. English bits and Welsh bits and Greek bits. Besides, I miss Mom."

"There you are," I said. "You say 'Mom' instead of 'Mum' just like an American girl."

"It means the same thing."

"It doesn't sound the same, though. And you'd miss Dad if you were living with us."

"I don't care. I've got to miss someone and Dad's just one person to miss. I wouldn't miss Barbie and her beastly new baby. But if I go on living with them it won't just be Mom— *Mum*—that I'm missing. I'll be missing you, too."

"Aw, come off it," I said.

But I was pleased, all the same.

◆

I suppose I missed her too. It can be useful having a young sister to run errands for you. (Aliki had never done much of that but I had cherished hopes for the future.) When she first went to America it had felt as if I'd lost part of myself. Like an arm or a leg.

I was particularly glad she was there for the week after the funeral. At least she was someone to talk to. My mother threw the odd word in my direction but she was too taken up with Childhood Friend to have much time for her own tiresome children. Not that Aliki seemed to mind. She and my mother both seemed to think Tasso was wonderful. I couldn't see it myself, but I kept my mouth shut.

I must admit he didn't leave Aliki and me out of things. He took us all out to eat every day. A lot of the tavernas were closed and their owners had gone home to Athens for the winter, but there were plenty of places still open and noisy and crowded. Greeks like to go out for meals with their friends all the year round. They are great people for parties.

It was strange eating indoors with the windows misted up and the television chattering away in the corner, instead of sitting outside with paper tablecloths snapping in the wind and a blue sky above. In fact, being in Greece in the winter was strange altogether. The people in the town seemed scurrying and secretive; no one smiled. Even the sewing woman, a little, bent person who lived in a house so narrow that it wasn't much more than a crack between the houses on either side, didn't cackle with laughter when we met in the square as she did in the summer. Unless we were with Aunt Elena, she scowled at us as she passed. "It's as if she didn't recognize us," Aliki said. And then, "Perhaps that was why the people were horrible at the funeral. Perhaps that's just what Greek people are like in the winter. Perhaps they're cross because their houses are cold."

I thought it was probably just because we were summer people who had no business here in the winter. But Aunt Elena's house was certainly cold. Aunt Elena wore a thick black woollen shawl over her black dress and thick black stockings. And the room we were sleeping in at the top of the house had frost on the inside of the windows. Aliki said, "It smells *damp*, Aunt Elena," which was a stupid thing to say because Aunt Elena opened the windows to let the air in and so we were colder than ever.

There was a fire downstairs in the living room and I sat so close to it that I could feel my knees scorching through the thick stuff of my jeans. Aunt Elena said, "You don't eat enough, Plato, that is why you are cold. And you are skinny as an old chicken." She gave my right ear a sharp tug, which was painful but meant as a sign of affection. "If you don't eat, how do you think you will ever grow tall and strong like a man?" She let out a long hoot of laughter. Like a foghorn. Or the Loch Ness monster.

Since this was precisely the fear that was haunting me, I couldn't share the joke. I said, "Perhaps I'd better go outside and run about to get my blood circulating again. Otherwise I won't be *able* to eat. My digestive system will freeze up— like that Iron Age man they found in the glacier. They found bits of Iron Age food still in his stomach!"

I had made this up. But it sounded as if it might be true. And Aunt Elena seemed to believe me. She didn't understand my jokes any more than I appreciated hers. She said, "You are a clever boy, Plato. But a strong brain needs a strong body. Go and take a walk with Aliki. Climb up to the castle."

◆

There are eight hundred and sixty-two stone steps up to the castle. Aliki said, "I don't mind walking down but I'm not walking *up*. My legs would just *break*. Why don't we ask Tasso to drive us?"

I said we couldn't treat the Dear Childhood Friend like a taxi driver. But Aliki knew I was really saying that I didn't want to ask him for anything because I thought he was spending too much time with our mother.

She gave me a sort of sneaky and superior grin, and said, "I'd rather go and look at the Gypsies."

Aliki is potty about the Gypsies. When she was younger she used to dream about being a Gypsy the way some girls dream about being pop stars or princesses. Greek Gypsies are amazingly beautiful, with dark skins and dark eyes, and the women and girls wear bright, spangly clothes and a lot of glittery jewelry. Some of them are rich—Aunt Elena says there is a king of the Gypsies who lives in Argos in the Peloponnese in a grand house with servants—but most of them live in tents or old broken-down buses and earn money by picking oranges and potatoes and selling white plastic chairs. They beg from the tourists in summer, teaching their children to pretend to be hungry: little boys with wide, sad eyes and little girls with babies on their hips holding out small grubby hands. But if you give them anything, they never say thank you; they just laugh and run off. They are much too proud to be grateful.

"You can't go and look at Gypsies as if they were in a zoo," I said.

"We could just walk *past*, couldn't we? Please. Oh, *please*, Plato."

Aliki can be sweet sometimes. Even if you know it's only because she wants you to do something, it's hard not to be taken in. I grumbled, of course. But we went.

There is a Gypsy camp outside Iria, on the marsh between the town's rubbish tip and the sea. It could be untidy and smelly in summer, but today the clean wind was coming straight off the water, blowing the stink of the rubbish inland, and I have to say that the tents, which were draped with bright warm rugs for the winter, looked quite romantic even to me.

Aliki said, with a huge, sad sigh, "Oh, I do wish I could be a Gypsy and live in a tent like that. And go where I wanted whenever I liked."

"No bathrooms," I said. "No running water. No washing machine." I paused and gave her a deeply significant look. *"No TV!"*

That almost got to her. She bit her lip and frowned. But then she tossed her head bravely. "I wouldn't care!"

"They would care, though. These Gypsies are descended from an ancient Indian people. They wouldn't allow you to join them, not just like that. You'd have to prove you were of the Blood."

I thought this was probably true. It sounded convincing to me.

Aliki squinted at me suspiciously. "I could *marry* one of them, couldn't I? Then it wouldn't matter that I wasn't an Indian. If I married a Gypsy prince."

But she was sounding more doubtful. Several boys who had been hanging around outside the tents had begun to slouch in our direction, and none of them looked exactly like princes, let alone future husbands.

"You said, 'Let's walk past'!" I reminded Aliki. "Not, 'Let's stand and stare.'"

I didn't want any more stones chucked at me. Though there didn't seem anything personal about the way the boys were scowling at us. Just a general warning to get off their patch. Which was fair enough. We had only come snooping. We had no real business here.

Other Gypsies were coming out of the tents now, the men in their dark clothes and the women and girls in their floaty and spangly dresses. None of them looked particularly menacing. Just not very friendly. But the dogs began barking.

I said, "We should have come by the road. Not along by the sea."

On the road there were people passing, in cars and on donkeys. But the road was on the other side of the camp. And the Gypsy boys had been moving around us so that now they were between us and the sea. The only clear way of escape was where the gulls were wheeling and crying.

I said, "We'll have to go over the rubbish tip."

Aliki pulled a sick face. She said, "*Gross.* I'd rather *die.* I'm not afraid of those idiot boys!"

"Nor am I," I said, lying a bit, but not much. I was fairly sure the boys would only crowd us and tease us if we tried to walk past them. Not exactly agreeable but not dangerous, either.

I said, "We ought to go. We're trespassing. I mean this bit of marsh belongs to them. Not really, I suppose, not legally, but they've always made a camp here. So it's just as if we were walking into someone's back garden."

Aliki said, a bit wistfully, "I don't expect they would really kidnap us, do you?"

"What for? I should think they've got enough silly girls to look after."

As if they had heard me, some of the girls were coming toward us. Except for one or two little ones, perched on a hip or clinging to a sequined skirt, they were mostly about Aliki's age, just as soft-faced and pretty if a bit dirtier. They paid no attention to me; they were after Aliki. They surrounded her with giggly cries and fluttery hands, stroking and patting and plucking and pinching.

Aliki said nothing, made no sound, but she had flushed scarlet with misery. Since she had been so keen to be a Gypsy herself I let her suffer a bit before I went to the rescue. One girl, older than the others, with breasts bursting her blouse and a dark moustache sprouting, had her brown fingers twisted in Aliki's long hair and was tugging it. Half playful, half spiteful. I saw tears in Aliki's eyes and pushed through to her. Dark Moustache stamped on my foot and jabbed her elbow into my throat. It hurt and I hit her.

That was a mistake. Not that I could have helped it, but a mistake all the same. Dark Moustache let out a yell, then put two of her long, grubby fingers into her mouth and let out a whistle so piercing that I could feel my eardrums contract with the pain. And the dogs began barking again.

The girls took off like a flock of bright birds. The adults, the men and the women, had disappeared into the tents. The boys behind us were laughing. And the dogs were running toward us.

They were wild-looking dogs, grayish and black, underfed, scrawny. And *fast*—no chance that we could run faster.

Aliki clutched the top of my arm, digging her nails in. I

[51]

said, "Just stand still. Don't be afraid. If we keep still they won't hurt us."

I didn't believe this for a minute. And it wasn't much comfort when they did stop a few yards away and started to circle around us, heads lowered, growling. *Licking their lips,* I thought, *waiting for the smell of fear to ripen their appetite.* Like the smell of bacon cooking.

I started to laugh inside in the way you do sometimes when something awful is happening. And it made me feel bolder. At least they weren't already upon us and chomping bits out of us. Then I remembered a film I had seen of hunting dogs tearing a live stag to pieces and stopped finding anything funny in this situation.

I whispered to Aliki, "Start to walk backward slowly. They'll only defend the camp. Just the perimeter. Once we're outside it, perhaps on the rubbish tip, they won't follow us."

I hoped this was true. Certainly, like not running away, it seemed to work. At least to begin with. While we stood still, the dogs stopped their circling. Then as we moved, they moved too, just as slowly. The leading dog sank to its stomach and, as we stepped backward, rose to its feet and walked forward. When we stopped, it lay down again.

"Grandmother's Footsteps," Aliki said shakily.

"Or, What's the Time, Mr. Wolf?"

I shouldn't have said it. I find that kind of awful joke helpful. It seems to steady me. But it had a dire effect on Aliki. She let out a wobbly, rising moan, let go my arm, and turned to run, stumbling toward the rubbish tip.

The dogs didn't move at once, just started a low, savage snarling. I could see the hairs standing stiff on their backs.

Then two of them crouched belly-to-earth and began to run forward. Gathering speed. Ready to spring.

Things like this take longer to write than to happen. The dogs were coming toward me; I was too scared to move. I stood, frozen and terrified. Then they swerved away suddenly, changing direction, and I knew it wasn't me they were after. They were chasing the silly, terrified creature who had been stupid enough to run away from them. They were hunters, and they were hunting Aliki.

I suppose I might have been relieved for a second. But to be honest I don't remember what I felt, only what I did. And there was nothing brave in what I did because it was an instinctive reaction. As Uncle Emlyn says, any fool can be brave if he doesn't have time to think.

I was on the edge of the rubbish tip. I picked up a squashed tin can and threw it as hard as I could at the nearest dog. I am useless at ball games, so it was luck that I caught its gray snout, and luck that the tin was sharp or heavy enough to be painful.

The dog gave a shrill, startled yelp. I threw another tin at the second dog, then a broken green bottle. I could hear Aliki screeching away like one of the gulls that swooped overhead, but the dogs had stopped chasing her. I walked backward, picking up bits of stinking rubbish to hurl at the dogs, expecting them to attack any minute and sink their teeth into me.

But none of them followed me onto the tip. It seemed I'd been right to think it was outside the bounds of the camp. Once those dogs had chased us off, they reckoned they'd done their job. I watched them loping back to the tents, now and then frisking their back legs as if they were feeling pretty cheerful and pleased with themselves.

I wasn't *dis*pleased with myself either. At least Aliki and I were not immediately doomed to play central roles in another Greek funeral. Finding yourself alive when you might easily have been dead does give a lift to the spirits. I whistled a bit as I plodded over the tip, keeping my eyes on the ground to avoid the soggiest patches, though there was no way of escaping the disgusting stink. Mostly rotting fishbones, I decided, though every now and again I got a whiff of something even older and nastier, so foul and putrid that I tried to stop breathing. It made me pick my way even more carefully. Scared of falling facedown in this muck.

As my dear little sister had done. I hadn't seen her fall because the rubbish tip rose up in the middle and she was over the top, out of my sight, but I hadn't been worried; I could hear her wailing in a steady, determined way that meant she was angry and outraged, but perfectly safe. And when I came over the ridge, there she was, on the far side of the tip, slimed head to foot with dead fish and feathered with pieces of plastic, her face scarlet, her mouth square with crying, knuckling her fingers into her eyes like a much younger child, a little baby of about six or seven instead of a girl of eleven who was unnaturally tall for her age.

Of course she was not putting on this revolting performance for me. It was Tasso who was getting the benefit. He was standing beside her, dabbing at her fairly uselessly with what had once been a clean handkerchief and muttering over and over, "There, Princess, there, please stop crying, it is not so dreadful. . . ."

Which was not what he thought, I could see. His mouth

[54]

was pursed with distaste. His Mercedes was on the road beside him, the driver's door wide open as if he had got out in a hurry, the white leather seat gleaming. Well, at least the back seat was covered with plastic.

For the first time I felt friendly toward him. A rush of fellow feeling, anyway. And obviously he had no idea how to cope with Aliki.

I said, "Do shut up, Al. You're safe, it's all *over.*" And, because I was still feeling pleased with myself, even proud, just a little, and wanted Tasso to know it, I added, "I got rid of the dogs. You ran away and so they ran after you but I managed to stop them."

I grinned at Tasso. I don't know what I expected. Praise for my selfless courage? A medal for Plato-the-Hero? If so, I was stupid.

Tasso said, "Why did you bring her to this filthy place, Plato? You are older, you should know better. A boy should take better care of his sister."

CHAPTER · 5

My Welsh grandmother says the Greeks spoil their male children. I can only say that is not my experience.

Aliki sat in the back of the car. Her angry wails had subsided to occasional sad little hiccups and snuffles. I sat in the front, beside Tasso, and tried to explain what had happened. He said, "Even if it was your sister's idea in the first place, you should not have allowed it. It is a man's job to protect women. Has your father not taught you this lesson?"

I could think of a good many answers to this but I said nothing. Why should I bother? I didn't care what this rich Greek thought of me! This rich *stupid* Greek! He couldn't be very intelligent or it might have occurred to him that my father hadn't exactly worn himself to the bone protecting my mother!

I turned my head away and stared sternly out of the window. Tasso put on a cassette of Greek bazouki music and turned it up loud. But I could still hear Aliki snuffing and snorting behind me.

I felt almost like crying myself. There was a bump in the back of my throat. But I thought of what Tasso would say if I did and that stopped me.

When we got to the square, he said, "You had better go and prepare your mother, I think."

He flashed his gold tooth at me, grinning away as if he had suddenly decided we were the best of old friends. I didn't demean myself by smiling back, just lifted my eyes to heaven to show that I shared his wry amusement at what was certain to be my mother's reaction when she saw Aliki. Tasso's smile faded at once, but it wasn't until I was halfway up the marble steps of Aunt Elena's house that I remembered that to a Greek, raising your eyes meant "No": "I don't have. I don't want." It was as if I had said to Tasso, "I won't do what you say."

He must have thought I was being disgustingly rude. I groaned loudly and struck my forehead with the back of my hand as I went into the house, and Aunt Elena, coming out of the kitchen, looked at me in amazement. "What is wrong, Plato? Are you not well?"

I could have said, "Just embarrassed," but it didn't seem the moment to go into the differences between English and Greek body language.

I said, "Aliki fell on the rubbish tip. I'm afraid she smells horrible."

Aliki had already appeared in the doorway. Aunt Elena screamed with horror and threw her hands up. Her words rattled out, fast and sharp. "Oh, Aliki, what have you done?

Oh, I am glad your mama has gone to the post office! Why should you fall on the rubbish? You are not hurt, not cut anywhere? If you are, we must go straight to the hospital. There must be an injection for antitetanus. No, no—you must not come into the house. We will take your clothes off in the storeroom. Oh, you naughty girl, what trouble you make for us.''

After the way Tasso had spoken to me I wasn't sorry to see Aliki getting the blame from someone. But it was hard on her all the same. Especially when Aunt Elena took hold of her arm like a policeman and marched her down the marble steps, calling over her shoulder, "Plato, we will need two buckets. I have one in the storeroom. You must fetch the one from the kitchen.''

I found a bucket beneath the stone sink and met Tasso outside the front door. I hoped he had heard Aunt Elena's blast of anger against Aliki. I smiled politely and said, "I couldn't tell my mother because she has gone to the post office. If you see her, perhaps you will warn her. I've got to help Aunt Elena.''

Because the house was built into the side of the mountain, the storeroom had no windows at the back, and only one at the side that would have looked out on the square if it had not been tightly shuttered. The door to this half-basement room was beneath the marble steps at the front of the house, in the garden. Aunt Elena had left this heavy door open to let the light in. Aliki's clothes lay in a stinking pile on the wooden floor and she stood, naked and wet and whimpering, in a tin bath. As I came in Aunt Elena threw another bucket of water over her and Aliki squealed with the shock of it.

"You must be brave, Aliki," Aunt Elena said. "It will soon be over and you can have a hot bath and clean clothes, and be comfortable. Plato, fill your bucket from the tap in the wall and put Aliki's things to soak in the water. We do not want your mother to come home and find all this trouble."

"I'm f-f-freezing," Aliki said. She was shaking and shivering. "I c-c-can't b-b-bear it."

"Think of CLJ," Aunt Elena said unexpectedly. And then, as if we didn't know who he was, "CLJ, your Welsh grandfather. He was many weeks here, just this cold water to wash in, and no natural light, and most of the time in a hole under the floor. When I say 'most of the time' I mean twenty-three hours out of twenty-four. Think of that, of the dark and the loneliness and the danger, and try to be just a little bit like your grandfather."

Aliki was still shivering. But she had stopped whimpering. She watched Aunt Elena fill the bucket and made no sound when the icy water struck her. She said, "I've never seen where you hid him. You showed Plato once, he told me you did, but you never showed me."

"I expect you were too young," Aunt Elena said. "Just one more bucket and you will be clean enough to go into the house. Plato, stir her clothes around in the water. It will loosen the worst of the dirt and then they can go into the washing machine. Are you ready, Aliki? *Whoosh*—there, my lamb, that's all over. I will give you something to cover you. Sometimes I wash myself here when I've been in the garden."

She took a toweling robe from a hook on the wall and wrapped it around Aliki. She gave her a thump on the shoulder in her rough sort of way that was meant to be loving.

[59]

"Now," she said, "perhaps you would like to eat or drink something?"

"I'd like to see where you hid CLJ." Aliki spoke in the sort of voice that says, "I've been good, so you owe me."

"Your mother might come back," Aunt Elena said.

◆

That was another unexpected remark. But I was only surprised for a minute. Of course Aunt Elena would know how my mother felt about my father's family. My mother said it was my Welsh grandmother's fault our father had left us, and although I didn't think this could be true, or at least not the whole story, it was what she had made up her mind to believe. But she had never said anything nasty about CLJ, and I had thought she was pleased for people to know that Aliki and I were his grandchildren. As if his being famous made us a bit famous, too.

On the other hand, CLJ was the reason why my mother and father had met in the first place. My father had come here, to this house, to meet the family who had saved CLJ, and had fallen in love with my mother and married her. The way things had turned out between them, she might not want to come back to find us exploring a bit of old history she would rather forget.

I said, "Tasso has gone to look for her. I expect he'll take her somewhere for a drink or a coffee. So we've got time."

Aunt Elena nodded. She was tapping her front teeth with her forefinger and her thin, fierce face was softer-looking than usual, and thoughtful.

She said, "There are things you should know. It is wrong to keep secrets from children."

I wondered what secrets she meant. But before I could ask her she had pushed the tin bath aside and was bending to a rusty iron ring in the floor, brushing the dirt away from it.

Then she straightened her back. She said, "When the Germans moved in we covered this place with a barrel of retsina. Sometimes a German officer would come with a jug to fetch the wine and would stay here, drinking and laughing with me. And I would sometimes take a glass with him and laugh at his jokes, making as much noise as I could because I was always afraid CLJ would start coughing. He had a sickness in his lungs from the dampness under the floor." She smiled at me. "Could you lift the trap, Plato? I am getting old and my back pains me sometimes."

It was very stiff, very heavy. I know there is no special virtue in being a hulk and enormously strong, but I wanted to show Aunt Elena that I wasn't as puny and miserable as she seemed to think me. And although to start with I thought the effort was going to tear my arms from my shoulders, once I had the trapdoor halfway up it was easier. I thought there was probably a mathematical way of explaining this, something about the division of gravity-pull between two sides of a triangle, and decided to ask Uncle Emlyn the next time I saw him.

Aliki said in an incredulous voice, "*No one* could live in that hole for a minute!"

I let the door gently down on the floor and went to join her. There was a smell of cold earth. The space under the floorboards was rectangular, shallower at one end than the other because the foundations of the house had been leveled into the mountain behind it.

"It's really *creepy*," Aliki said. "Can I get in, Aunt Elena?"

[61]

She didn't wait for an answer. She slid in at the shallow end. At the deep end, the earth rose to her shoulders. She said, "If you put the lid down, I couldn't stand up. And CLJ is taller than I am."

I said, "Shall I shut you in? Then you'll know what it must have been like."

Aliki had gone very pale. She said, "I can tell without that. I can imagine myself into the dark." She looked at Aunt Elena and spoke as if she were pleading with her to let her off. "I couldn't have borne it. I know I would die."

Aunt Elena said, "People can sometimes do things when they have to. Things they would not have thought of beforehand as possible. You and Plato will be brave people, Aliki, because CLJ is in you. Is part of you both."

Aliki jumped up and sat on the side of the hole. "I suppose some light would have come through the floorboards? Did he have blankets and pillows?"

Aunt Elena was watching her. She wasn't smiling with her mouth but there was a smile in her eyes. "I made it as comfortable as I could. He had a little bread, and fruit sometimes, and always water and wine. And when I came at night, when the German soldiers were sleeping, I brought him our Greek newspapers and a radio that belonged to one of our neighbors so that he could listen to your English BBC. He could straighten his legs and exercise his body and whisper a little to me. I could tell him things that were not in the newspapers. The hall of the house and the stairs are directly above us and the ceiling is thin. If anyone came down we would hear them."

"What about him going to the lavatory?" Aliki asked.

She gave me a sly look. She was at the age when the idea

of important or powerful people—our grandfather, her teacher, the Queen—performing their natural functions was a bit of a giggle.

Aunt Elena answered her calmly. "I made arrangements, Aliki. I was a young girl and shy, but when it is a matter of life and death modesty is not so important. And since we all had so little to eat, none of us could open our bowels very often. That made the question of disposal very much easier."

Aliki was blushing furiously. I said, "There you are! Serves you right!"

"What are you talking about, Plato dear?" Aunt Elena said. She knew perfectly well, because she went on, without waiting. "Now, Aliki, I think it is time you should take a warm bath. Your mother will be back soon and if she finds you like this she will be afraid you catch cold."

"It's *might* catch cold," Aliki corrected her, annoyed because Aunt Elena had embarrassed her. "You make a lot of mistakes, Aunt Elena."

"Thank you, my lamb. I am always happy to learn. When I make the mistakes, I hope you will tell me."

This politeness, which was really teasing, made Aliki blush again. She stomped out of the storeroom, the toweling robe brushing the ground behind her. Aliki might be tall, but Aunt Elena was taller. Exceptionally tall for a woman.

I thought, *If CLJ had married Aunt Elena, if he hadn't been married to my tiny Welsh grandmother, I might be going on six foot by now.*

She was emptying the bath into a drain in the corner of the room. I said to her back, "You said secrets. What is the *secret?*"

She hung the bath on a hook on the wall. She didn't answer me. I thought, *Playing deaf?*

I said, "I mean, the hole under the floor wasn't a secret. Even if Aliki had never seen it before. I mean, we both *grew up* on that story! Dad says CLJ told him that during the war he lived in a cave, and when he was very young Dad used to think that must be ages ago, hundreds of years, like the Stone Age."

Aunt Elena gave a funny laugh—in fact more of a sudden sigh, and a breathless gulp, and a kind of heave as if she was having a fight with herself not to cry, but "funny laugh" is the best way to describe it. I know that as she turned round to face me she was smiling and her eyes were bright.

She said, "Oh, yes, it was a long time ago."

I said—I don't know what made me say it—"I wish *you* were my grandmother."

She did laugh then. A deep chuckle in the back of her throat. She said, "I think we have things to talk about, you and I, Plato. Close the trapdoor. Wait for me in the square."

◆

I sat on the edge of the old Turkish fountain. The stone was warm from the sun that had been shining all afternoon, and because the little square was out of the cold winter wind I began to feel sleepy. I must have closed my eyes because Aunt Elena was suddenly standing in front of me. She was carrying a basket. She wore a black scarf on her head. She said, "Well? Are you coming?"

I said, "I wasn't asleep. Is Mum back? Is she angry?"

Aunt Elena shook her head. "She is happy with Tasso."

It wasn't exactly an answer but I understood what she

meant all the same. In some ways Aunt Elena is like Uncle Emlyn. Or my best friend, Jane Tucker. Three people I can talk to in shorthand.

Aunt Elena set off up the marble stairs at the side of the fountain that led to the upper town. Since the old town is built on the side of the mountain it is all steep steps and climbing. My mother says everyone in Iria develops leg muscles like iron. Even very old people seem to soar up like birds. And Aunt Elena, who isn't as old as all that, who is younger than CLJ, left me panting and groaning.

She was waiting at the top of the second flight. She said, "You get used to it. If I leave Iria for just a short week I am like you when I come back. Out of breath. Aching."

"It's just asthma with me. Are we going much higher?"

"To the top. Under the walls of the castle. But we can rest here a little."

We sat on a stone seat under a fig tree. We could see the battlements of the castle above us and the flat sea below. The wind must have dropped because the water was silky and still. And the mountains on the other side of the great bay were misty.

I think descriptions are boring but there are times when I wish I could paint. I would like to paint Iria.

I said, "Where did the submarine pick him up? It couldn't have been in the harbor. There must have been soldiers watching."

"Oh, yes," Aunt Elena said. "Soldiers everywhere. Iria was a garrison town. But the British got CLJ out all the same." She gave her deep chuckle. "Under the nose of the Germans."

She was quiet for a minute. She looked as if she was happy,

[65]

remembering. Then she said, "My Uncle Cleon had a small fishing boat. He took CLJ out of the harbor hidden under his nets. The Germans would search the boats in the usual way but Cleon had been generous with gifts. Fresh fish. Sometimes even a lobster."

I said, "There's a saying. 'Beware the Greeks bearing gifts.' Your uncle couldn't be certain they wouldn't look under the nets. Would they have shot him?"

"Yes. Certainly."

"And you? If they found out you were hiding a spy, they would have shot you as well, wouldn't they?"

"I expect so." She chuckled again. "It was not something to think of. People risked their lives all the time. It was just the way we lived then."

I said, "I don't understand my grandmother. I mean, she's CLJ's *wife*. She says she hates the Greek people because one of them told the Germans about the cave where he was hiding. But it was you *rescued* him, you and your Uncle Cleon. So she ought to *love* you. All of your family."

I meant, *And my mother, too. She ought to love my mother.* But I didn't say it.

Aunt Elena looked straight ahead. The black scarf covered her hair and made her face look extra beaky and bony. She said, "My older sister married the man who told the Germans where he was hiding. That was your mother's mother. Your Greek grandmother. She married Nikos Petropoulos."

⊛CHAPTER · 6

People as old as Aunt Elena, as old as my grandparents, talk about the Second World War as if they were still living through it. As if nothing exciting or interesting had taken place between then and now. It doesn't seem to occur to them that hearing their stories over and over might be dull for the rest of us.

I once said something like this to Uncle Emlyn. I was staying in Wales and CLJ was giving an interview. Part of a program for the BBC. The house was stuffed with sound men and cameramen and the street outside was solid with buses and catering vans. "Television crews march on their tiny stomachs," Uncle Emlyn said. "They have to be fed every few hours, just like babies."

I think I said it was all a bit silly. I meant, all this fuss about something that had taken place back in the Dark Ages. I was going through a phase when I thought most grown-up preoccupations were fairly foolish if not downright des-

picable. Uncle Emlyn must have asked what I meant—
"Define that remark," was how he probably put it. And
somehow I got to the point where I said it was a terrible
thing that poor old men like CLJ should have nothing to talk
about except that long-ago war. As if nothing exciting had
happened to them since they had all that fun killing each
other.

Uncle Emlyn said it was a fair point to make, so I knew
he was about to disagree with me. He said, "They were all
young then, laddie, that's partly what they remember. But
that's not the whole of it."

We were walking up the steep hill that leads out of the
valley town where my grandparents live to the grassy top
of the mountain. (The one thing my Greek and Welsh families have in common seems to be a masochistic passion for
vertical living.) Uncle Emlyn, who is asthmatic like me, was
beginning to grunt. He stopped to recover but he was still
huffing a bit when he said, "Wars give ordinary people a
chance to be more than just ordinary. Going to work on a
bus or a train and going back home to sleep in front of the
telly doesn't give you a chance to be much of a hero—or
not in a dramatic way, anyway. Not in the sort of way that
quickens the pulses."

He leaned against a dry-stone wall and stuffed his puffer
in his mouth and sprayed away for a minute. He said wheez-
ily, "War sharpens things up. More black and white and less
gray. Less time for fudge and fossicking. Less awful con-
fusion about what's right and what's wrong. Your choices
get simpler. You can save your friend's life. Or betray him."

◆

I expect he went on after that the way he usually did, adding and subtracting, saying things like "On the other hand" and "Of course there are always exceptions"—Uncle Emlyn can never leave an idea *alone*. But what I remembered as I sat under the fig tree, high up in the old town of Iria, looking out at the sea and listening to Aunt Elena, was the bit about choices being simple in wartime.

This is the story Aunt Elena told me.

Nikos Petropoulos was born in Molo, in the village where we saw him buried, and lived there until he was sixteen, when he went to Germany to work in a restaurant. That was sometime in the middle thirties, so Aunt Elena thought. Sixty years ago.

Nikos learned German, worked as a waiter, and sent money home to his parents. Then his father died and he came home to look after his mother. The war broke out and for a year he was in the army, but he stepped on a mine fighting the Italians in Albania and was discharged with half his foot missing. When the Germans invaded and occupied Molo he looked for a new way of fighting the enemy.

No one else in the village spoke German. He made himself useful to the German commandant, acting as an interpreter, taking him presents: honey from his bees, apricots from his mother's garden. He pretended to be a bit simpleminded, a result of his war wound. The commandant was a man who liked to make himself comfortable and Nikos was still a good waiter; sometimes, when the commandant entertained fellow officers, Nikos was asked to serve at the table. He stood well back in the shadows. And he kept his ears open.

There was a band of guerrillas somewhere in the wooded mountains above the village. And Nikos, of course, knew the mountains as well as he knew his mother's garden. When he was young, he and his friends had found several deep channels running down the mountainside, dried-up torrents that were hidden now, camouflaged by scrub and trees. They had played in a particularly deep cave, the Cave of the Prophet Elias, just under the peak of the mountain, that was big enough for a shepherd to shelter his sheep and goats in if the weather turned nasty. And big enough to make a good base for guerrillas.

Everyone knew about the guerrillas, including the Germans, but only a few shepherds knew how to find them, and the shepherds kept well away from the village in case it should enter the commandant's head to ask questions. The boys who sometimes took food and wine up the mountain and left it in a grove of chestnut trees behind a ruined temple were too young to make the Germans suspicious. If they were stopped, they could say they were taking food to a brother or sister who was minding the family sheep.

Older people leaving the village were likely to be watched more closely. Especially if they were away long enough to make their way through the forest to the top of the mountain. But the channels that Nikos remembered went straight up and were a fairly easy climb, even for a man with a damaged foot. Besides, Nikos was known to be a bit soft in the head. And the commandant was fond of mushrooms.

Nikos took him a full basket one evening. They made a good dish cooked with oil and garlic and herbs, and the commandant slurped them up eagerly. Nikos pretended to be delighted. He was glad to have found something to tempt the commandant's appetite. (It could have been a touch dangerous to be quite so smarmy if the commandant had not been thick as several planks as well as hugely fat and greedy.)

Nikos promised to get the good commandant more of the mushrooms. The best, unfortunately, were to be found deep in the forest. But he would find the time somehow.

The guerrillas were in the Cave of the Prophet Elias, as Nikos had guessed. Although they were supplied with arms by this time, largely due to CLJ and his radio, they were short of warm clothes and boots. They wore leather slippers or slices of rubber tire fastened with wire. But they were in high good spirits. They had just blown up a bridge and derailed a German supply train.

Nikos had a few tidbits of news for them that they couldn't have got on their radio—scraps of conversation overheard from the commandant's table or hanging round the soldiers in the taverna. Rumors of troop movements, that sort of thing. Then he had to go back, on the way picking the mushrooms. His alibi.

The next time he went, the guerrillas had questions ready. Some of them, like the exact size of this or that garrison, he couldn't answer. Someone—it could even have been CLJ—suggested that it would be very useful if he could get himself a job in the commandant's office. To do that he would have to come up with a more imposing present than a basket of mushrooms. The Allied forces were making an arms drop in a field on the far side of Iria. The guerrillas would make sure they got there first, they couldn't afford to lose the guns and ammunition, but they would make it look as if they had left in a hurry, as if the Germans would have caught them had they come an hour earlier. So it would appear to be a genuine tip-off.

And so it began, and went on. Nikos, the go-between,

trading secrets. The balance of advantage was naturally on the Greek side. One day, Nikos even managed to release two members of the Resistance from the prison in Iria by slipping the orders into a pile of other papers waiting for the commandant's signature at the end of a busy day.

CLJ was in the news by now. The Germans, busy making him into Chief Bogeyman, credited him with even more success than he had actually had. The commandant, who had never heard of Wales until now, said it was well known that Welshmen were diabolically clever. And Nikos realized that he was talking about the foreigner who was living with the guerrillas in the Cave of the Prophet Elias. The foreigner who was his friend.

The German soldiers were very bored in the small village of Molo. A little looting and burning would have cheered them up, but the commandant, in spite of being greedy and stupid and lazy, was a good disciplinarian. They would have sat out the rest of the war in that village with no harm coming to anyone if one of the soldiers, rather more bored than the others, had not attacked a young shepherdess, driving her ewes home from the next valley. The priest found her, weeping and bleeding at the side of the road, took her home to her family, and complained—through Nikos— to the commandant, who was shocked and apologetic. He promised to deal with the soldier severely, but when he sent for him he was missing and when he was finally found he was dead. The girl's brothers, who were with the guerrillas, had come down from the mountain and killed him.

They had beaten him with an iron bar. They had pulled out his toenails. When he fainted, they threw cold water over him to revive him. Then they cut him, crisscross cuts

[72]

all over his body. They had no salt to rub into the cuts so they rolled him in a patch of thistles, slashed an artery, and left him to bleed to death slowly.

The commandant had daughters of his own. If the soldier had been killed cleanly, shot through the forehead, he might have been able to avoid taking hostages. But this was a death he couldn't let pass.

The soldiers rounded up the old men and the little boys, who were the only males left in Molo, and locked them in the church. The oldest man was eighty-four, the youngest boy three and a half. (There was a younger boy baby in Molo, in the family with whom Elena was living, but the soldier who searched the house pretended not to see him.)

The commandant ordered the women to gather in the main square and, through Nikos, told them that unless the men who had killed the soldier were handed over by the next morning, he would hang the hostages from the plane tree outside the taverna and set fire to the village.

Nikos pleaded with the commandant. He had seen photographs of two pretty girls on his desk, also one of a chubby boy about five years old. The commandant ignored him. Nikos walked around Molo, listening to the women's cries from the dark houses and to the little boys sobbing inside the locked church.

He must have felt his heart was breaking.

Nikos woke his mother before the dawn broke. Then he went to the commandant's lodgings. The commandant was already awake; perhaps he hadn't slept either. Nikos told him the price he was ready to pay for his village, and the commandant accepted enthusiastically. His superiors would rather have the Chief Bogeyman than a tree hung with dead

[73]

Greeks and a few burned Greek houses. He believed Nikos; he thought he was too much of a fool to tell lies. But to make sure, he locked him up in the guardroom.

By this time his mother had gone to the house where Elena was staying and sent her to the Cave of the Prophet Elias.

◆

Aunt Elena said, "Nikos knew that my parents had a safe house in Iria and would hide CLJ until the British could come for him. He thought also that, if things went wrong and he was in trouble himself, it would be best for me if I was out of the village because of the connection between us. He was already betrothed to my sister, you see. To your mother's mother. Although they did not get married until two years later."

My head was spinning. There seemed to be a huge dark aching hole in my stomach. I said, "He couldn't have known you would get there in time."

Aunt Elena lifted her eyes in the Greek sign for *no*. "I think he thought I would not. But it was all he could think of. The best he could do. It was luck that I found the way quickly. And I had good strong legs then."

She was watching me with a sad, grave expression. "Not all the guerrillas were so lucky. Most of them escaped into the mountains but the Germans caught two of them. They brought them down to the village and shot them in the square."

My mouth was dry. "What happened to Nikos?"

She laughed in an angry way. "What do you think, Plato? The commandant wanted CLJ. He guessed Nikos knew where he was. Of course, Nikos would not say. Even when he was

[74]

tortured. But the village never forgave him. Two of their young men had been shot. And in betraying CLJ, he had shamed them. They should have defended him with their lives. Nikos had betrayed their honor as Greeks."

I said, "But he *saved* them. The soldiers would have burned down the village. And hanged all the men!"

Aunt Elena laughed again, a proper laugh now. "That didn't happen. So it was forgotten. Except by a few." She stood up very suddenly, smoothing her black skirt, picking up her basket. She said, "You must never sit too long under a fig tree. Its shadow is heavy and there are many dark spirits."

"You don't believe that!" I said.

She didn't answer me. Just looked at me sidelong with a little smile twitching her lips.

My Welsh grandmother says all Greeks are superstitious. It is a religion with them, she says, sniffing and pursing her mouth up in a superior way.

But I never know with Aunt Elena. She might just have decided to change the subject.

I said, "There were some people who came to the funeral. To the house, I mean, and the church."

"Women. The women who had cause to thank him. It is always the men who think so much about honor. Now we are to climb a long stair and you will need all your breath."

I said, "*Wait* a minute. Why did he stay in the village? He could have gone somewhere else."

She made an impatient gesture and started up the steep flight of steps. She shouted over her shoulder, "Why should he run away? Molo was his village. His home."

I thought she said something else but we had climbed up into the wind again and I couldn't hear. The wind blew into

[75]

my mouth; I leaned forward against it and it was strong as a wall. Aunt Elena was at the top a good couple of minutes before me. She said, "No more climbing."

We were in a narrow street with a crumbling stone wall on one side and an enormous derelict house on the other. The roof was a blackened skeleton at one end and, looking through the gaping holes where there had once been windows, I could see that most of the floors were no longer there. But I was not altogether surprised, when Aunt Elena knocked on a little, low door, to hear a cracked old voice calling inside; a lot of people live in ruined houses in Iria. In the cellars, or perched like birds on a rickety upper floor.

The door opened into a dark room furnished with stiff-looking chairs and sofas and a lot of heavy carved furniture lining the walls. In the middle of the room there was the biggest television set I had ever seen in my life, and sitting in front of it, about three feet from the screen, an old woman in a high-backed chair. She was wearing black, as old Greek women do, and beneath her black head scarf her grayish face was wrinkled up in solid humps and hollows like a map made from papier-maché.

Aunt Elena put her basket down on a table beside the old woman, who peeked under the white cloth and let out a stream of gratitude and amazement and mock reproach that I guessed could have been translated into any language as meaning, "Oh, you shouldn't have done it!"

Aunt Elena took her hands and kissed her on the stiff contours of both cheeks and turned to me. She said, "Plato, this is my good friend, Kyria Aphrodite."

I thought of the Greek goddess Aphrodite rising from the waves and wanted to laugh but I didn't. I shook Aphrodite's hand, which was warm and bony and quite nice to hold, though more like a monkey's paw than a human being's, and she hung on to mine while Aunt Elena introduced me with what sounded like practically a university lecture on consanguinity. As I think I've mentioned before, the Greeks are batty about family relationships.

I didn't understand a word she was saying until suddenly a whole sentence leapt out at me. Aunt Elena said, *"Enai o engonos tou Nikou Petropoulou."* I suppose I heard the *name*, even though it didn't sound quite right (I found out later that Aunt Elena was using the genitive case), and then guessed the rest: "He is the grandson of Nikos Petropoulos." But I was taken by surprise at the time. It was as if a light had been switched on. A key sentence highlighted on a computer screen.

Kyria Aphrodite was more than surprised. She gave a wild screech, as if something or someone had unexpectedly bitten her. She clutched my hand with both of hers and took it to her mouth and started mumbling at it. Kissing it. Then she held it to her throat and looked up at me, tears spurting out of her eyes and making a rather sluggish journey down the deep, curving channels in her cheeks, and started gabbling in Greek.

No more startling flashes of illumination. I had no idea at all what she was saying.

Until Aunt Elena interpreted. "Kyria Aphrodite comes from Molo. Her old father and her eight-year-old son were locked in the church and would have been hanged by the Germans. Nikos is a saint to her."

◆

I understood why she had taken me to visit this ancient person. It was supposed to make me feel better to meet someone who didn't think my Greek grandfather was scum. But I wasn't grateful. One old woman slobbering over me couldn't make up for all those men I had seen in the village standing still in the square as his coffin passed by. Silent. Unforgiving. Despising him for a traitor.

I felt horribly stupid. Humiliated. I had thought that my Welsh grandmother was spiteful and foolish to hate my mother. Blaming her so unreasonably just for being Greek. When all the time she did have a reason. My mother was the daughter of the man who betrayed CLJ to the Germans. It wasn't my mother's fault. She hadn't even been born then. But that wouldn't deter my Welsh grandmother. The Bible freak. Jones-the-Bible. *The sins of the fathers shall be visited on the children unto the third and fourth generation.*

I was surprised she seemed so keen on me and Aliki! I would have thought she wouldn't want to see either of us in the circumstances. I wondered how CLJ felt. Thinking about *that* brought back the aching, dark hole in my stomach.

Going home, I followed Aunt Elena down the first flight of steps. We had to go single file because the wind was behind us now, and we had to hold hard to the rusty iron rail in the wall to avoid being blown down rather faster than would have been comfortable. When we got to the fig tree, which was sheltered by a high wall, we stopped to draw breath.

She looked at me. I had the feeling she had been working out what to say. "Now you know, Plato. One day you must tell Aliki about the Greek side of your family. But not yet.

It is not yet as important to her as it is to you, I think. And I ask you, please do not speak about this to Maria."

That was all. I expected her to enlarge on why I shouldn't talk to my mother about her own father. But she gave her head a shake as if to say that was the end of the matter and was off down the next stairway before I could speak. Not that I had anything more to say. A mystery had been cleared up. I had wanted to know and been told. And I didn't feel any better for it.

That's a huge understatement. I felt a lot *worse*. It was as if I had found out I was someone else altogether. Or as if there was another person lurking inside me, someone I hadn't known about before and didn't much like now I knew him.

CHAPTER • 7

We went home. That is, Mum and I flew to England and
Aliki flew to New York. Aliki's plane left later than ours
and we had to go through Passport Control and leave her at
the barrier with Aunt Elena. Neither my mother nor Aliki
cried when we said goodbye. That was something to do with
Aunt Elena being there, probably. Most Greeks are given to
wailing and tearing their hair at emotional moments but
Aunt Elena is not one of them.

So we were all extremely stiff-upper-lip. Aliki had gone
very silent. That was worse in a way than howling and
screaming. I said, "We're all coming back in July, it's not
long till July." But she shook her head in a despairing way
as if the six months between then and now were a lifetime.

It would have been better if we could have stayed longer
together. Then we would have had time to get fed up with
each other. But Mum had to get back to the estate agent's
office. When she had said she must have a week's holiday

to go to Greece for the funeral, the man she worked for had pointed out that if she didn't want the job there were plenty who did.

I knew she wouldn't want to ask Dad for more money. Not that he would have much to spare when the Dentist-Doll had her baby. I remembered that my mother had not been given this joyful news yet.

She was looking sad enough without that, I thought, when we were strapped in our seats and waiting for takeoff. It couldn't be just because her father was dead. Perhaps being in Greece had reminded her of how she had met my dad and fallen in love with him. Getting married Romeo-and-Juliet style and then it all turning sour. (Shakespeare knew what he was doing when he finished *that* loving couple off. He knew if he let them live, Romeo would march out after a year or so and take up with someone else. Did they have dentists then?)

But she was probably more upset at this moment because of Aliki. And since I was a bit miserable about my giantess sister myself, I felt sympathetic. I said, "You going to have a drink when they come round? If you like, if they've got champagne on the trolley, I'll treat you." All other drinks are free on Olympic Airways.

She turned to me, big, soft, dark eyes misting over as if I'd offered her the moon. "Darling, that's sweet of you, but I'd really rather have orange juice."

Idiot that I am, I persisted. I said, "Aliki'll be all right, Mum, don't worry."

She dabbed her eyes with her handkerchief and smiled. Then said, as if I hadn't spoken, "I was just wishing that Tasso could have come to the airport instead of going to his

[81]

boring old meeting. Aren't I silly? When he's promised to come to London."

Sometimes I despair of my mother.

◆

I thought I would tell my friend Jane Tucker about Nikos Petropoulos as soon as I saw her. But when I rang her, which I did as soon as we got home that Saturday evening, it seemed too complicated to explain over the telephone. Besides, my mother was rushing from one room to the other doing what she called settling back in and, naturally, passing through the hall of our smallish flat about every thirty seconds or so.

When Jane and I were a bit younger we used to use Back-speak when we wanted to say something private, but although we still sometimes call each other Enaj and Otalp it is only as a sort of joke. And once you stop using a private language like that, you begin to forget it.

I could have made some excuse and gone out to the telephone box at the corner. Because my mother is terrified I will get lost when I'm out of her sight and need to get hold of her—or the police or the hospital—she makes me carry enough phone cards in my pocket to ring Vladivostok. The truth is, when it came to it I wasn't sure I wanted to tell Jane after all. I was feeling so bad about myself that I was afraid even someone like her might say something like, "Well of course, that's what's always been wrong with you!"

Bad blood. Sins of the fathers.

Obviously I didn't take after CLJ, the sainted family Hero. So I must take after the family Villain. No wonder I was runty and skinny and half blind and asthmatic. My Welsh grandmother had blamed the Greek in me and she had been right all the time.

Evil will out. My hideous physical appearance was the outward sign of my rotten inside: my treacherous character, my cowardly black heart. And admitting to something like that is like confessing that one of your immediate ancestors had a horrible and fatal disease like syphilis or Huntington's chorea. As it is, being seen with me doesn't do much for Jane's self-esteem.

So all I told her was that the funeral was a weird experience which I would be happy to share with her sometime. And that my baby sister wasn't so much a tall girl as a member of a different species. I thought of the first line of a hymn we sometimes sang when I went to church with my grandmother in Wales, "These things shall be, a loftier race." And laughed madly.

Jane said, "What's the matter?"

"Matter?" I said. "*Matter?*" And sang, "Oh, dear, what can the matter be?"

"Don't," she said. "Don't sing, Plato. Please."

Jane is not particularly musical herself, but she lives with a musical aunt (who teaches the piano and plays the drums) and I suppose it has made her sensitive. Though I must admit she is not the only person who has likened my singing to that of a hippopotamus in pain. And I have to admit that it is getting worse with the onset of puberty. An angry hippo who has smoked three packs of cigarettes a day for the last twenty years.

But because I was feeling so horrible, I took offense. "I can't help being handicapped," I said. "I suppose you think

[83]

people who are bad at dancing, who've got one leg shorter than the other, or perhaps are just ugly, shouldn't be allowed to try to dance in case the sight of them upsets other people. It's cruel to try and stop me singing just because I'm bad at it. I can't help being tone deaf." I thought of a fancier way of putting it. "Tonally deficient," I said. "Vocally disadvantaged."

"You poor thing," Jane said. "Hang on a minute." She must have covered the earpiece because although I knew she was calling out to one of the aunts her words were muffled and fuzzy. Then she said clearly, "Aunt Bill says, come to lunch tomorrow. Ask your mother if she'd like to come too. Aunt Bill says Maria won't want to bother cooking after a funeral, though what evidence she's got for that insightful remark I don't know."

She giggled. I could hear Aunt Bill shouting cheerfully in the background. I thought how nice it must be to live with people you can make silly jokes at, even be rude to in a friendly way, instead of walking on eggs all the time in order not to hurt their feelings.

◆

Jane has family problems too. (That is another story.) But she doesn't have to live with them as I have to live with my mother.

I'm not complaining. At that particular time of my life I was stuck with my mum. It was my job to look after her. All I am trying to say is that Jane's life is the perfect example of how much more comfortable life can be if you are not brought up by your parents.

That can't be absolutely true, of course. Or not what Uncle

Emlyn would call a universal law. But it applies to Jane and Aunt Bill and Aunt Sophie.

Aunt Bill is the painter. She paints huge, splashy pictures of growing things, not just trees and flowers but weeds—nettles and thistles. And she looks after the garden. Aunt Sophie, who is very small and rather fierce, does just about everything else. That is, when she isn't teaching the piano or traveling around the country playing the drums in a band. If you go to a meal at Jane's house you hope it is Aunt Sophie who is doing the cooking.

Both Aunt Bill and Aunt Sophie have things to do and think about that are important to them and so they don't weigh down on Jane the way my mother used to weigh down on me. (I suppose I really mean "concentrate on" but "weigh down on" is how it felt. Heavy.)

As you might expect, my mother thinks both Jane's aunts are pretty peculiar. "You must admit they are really rather eccentric" is what she says—usually with one of her silliest laughs. "But I suppose that's just because they are both so artistic."

I think she likes them, all the same, and I know they both tried to be nice to her. Aunt Bill put on a cleanish skirt and Aunt Sophie did her best to listen to what my mother was saying instead of just to the music she is always playing inside her own head.

It bothered me that they felt they had to try. As if my mother was some kind of alien from outer space instead of an ordinary person, not very clever, who had an unsatisfactory child to bring up on her own. Not a handsome hulk but a weedy little runt who couldn't see a thing without glasses and was no good at ball games.

[85]

She thought up a new thing to accuse me of at that lunch. She actually told Jane and the Aunts that I had fainted into the grave at her father's funeral.

"It was my fault!" she said. "I should never have taken him. It was rather a dreadful occasion. And Plato is such a sensitive boy."

It was clear from her tone that "sensitive" in her vocabulary was first cousin to "feeble."

The Aunts looked puzzled. Neither of them was able to see how "sensitive" could be used as an insult.

Jane wriggled her nose at me sympathetically. "I expect he didn't have any breakfast," she said. "I often faint at school if I don't eat in the morning."

Aunt Sophie said, "Jane!" But Aunt Bill laughed and winked at me.

I said, "Icrem Enaj," reckoning that not even Aunt Sophie would pick up French Backspeak. Jane pretended that she didn't understand either. She sighed and pulled one of her funny faces. Jane is the only person I have ever known who can cross her eyes *evenly*. So that they both almost disappear into the sides of her nose *at the same moment*.

I shall never get married. It leads to too much unhappiness. But if I were a marrying person, Jane would be the kind of girl I would go for.

◆

After lunch, Aunt Bill said she would drive my mum home when she was ready. So Jane and I went out for a while.

We live in a suburb of London. It has a Boots', a Woolworth's, a Marks and Spencer, and a Safeway's. Although there is a not-too-bad library, it doesn't open on Sundays.

[86]

There used to be several cinemas but they closed down because of television. Jane and I are too young to be admitted to one of the dozen or so public houses; I believe the idea is that it would corrupt people of our age to see our elders and betters getting drunk. And of course there is no café, nowhere you can sit down and have a cup of tea or a Coke. There is a McDonald's in the next suburb, but the local bus doesn't run on a Sunday afternoon and to get there by train you have to go all the way into London on the main line and out again.

In Iria, which is a much smaller town, there must be at least forty places where you can have a meal or an ice cream or a drink and talk to your friends. You can sit for as long as you like over one cup of coffee.

Deprived of these excitements, Jane and I went for a walk. There is some almost-country where the housing estates peter out: a rather *halfhearted* wood, a bit shabby and dusty, where people dump their dirty mattresses and stolen supermarket trolleys, and a few old gravel pits that have been filled in and are used for dinghy sailing. We stood on the edge of one of these pits to watch the boats with their red-nosed occupants tacking backward and forward. It seemed to me a limited and boring occupation. The water looked gray and slimy. It was very cold.

I said, "Whenever I come back from Greece I think what a dreary country this is." I went on to enlarge on the absence of cafés, cinemas, restaurants, and other manifestations of civilized life.

When I stopped to draw breath, Jane said coldly, "Why don't you go and live there if it's so marvelous."

I should have been warned. It was stupid to go into rap-

[87]

tures over a place she had never been to. I should have gone on to say that of course I liked England more, and thought of reasons why. But the only solid reason I could think of at that moment was that I couldn't speak Greek, and I didn't think that would be good enough. Just a sort of technical hitch.

So I said, "Because I don't belong. Really, I don't *belong* anywhere! Mum would like to go back and live in Greece but she can't because she's got me to bring up and educate and I wouldn't fit in there. But I don't fit in here either because I'm half Greek, so half of me wants to be in the sun and sit about in cafés laughing and talking. The other half, the Welsh half, is much sterner and gloomier. So I'm all mixed up—when I'm there I want to be here, and when I'm here I want to be there! It's as if I were split in two. And I don't now which half is *me*. The real me!"

This wasn't exactly true. Or I had only just thought of it. But it sounded impressive and I began to feel quite sorry for my sad plight.

I said, "It's just as bad for Aliki. Worse in a way. She seems like an all-American girl, the way she talks and everything, but she's got all the other bits too, deep inside, and I expect she'll have problems later. Feel confused, just like me."

Jane snorted. "You're not confused. You're pretending! All that 'Who am I?' stuff. Like some whiny brat!"

I should never have suggested that Iria might have some tiny advantages over our suburb. Jane looked very pretty when she was angry. I wasn't going to say so, I guessed it would make her really spit venom, but then she tossed her hair back and I couldn't help it.

[88]

I said, "You've got lovely hair. In spite of your warped personality."

I ducked in case she threw a punch at me. Instead, she gave me a sudden sharp, wise look and said, "What *happened* to you in Greece?"

I wondered how she knew. Female intuition, Uncle Emlyn would say. He's an old-fashioned sexist. He says women are incapable of rational thought.

Jane said, "Something did, didn't it?"

I nodded.

She said, "You don't have to tell me."

I had the horrible feeling that I was going to cry. I said, "Well, all sorts of things happened. I mean it stands to reason. You can't have a week with nothing happening, can you? Unless you spent all the time in a *coma*. Let me think! We went to a funeral—you heard my mother on that subject at lunch. What she didn't tell you was that I saved my young sister from being torn to pieces by savage dogs. And that she spent most of the time flirting with a rich Greek Aliki picked up on the plane. Someone my mother had known when they were both young, apparently."

Jane said reproachfully, "I did say you needn't tell me what happened. Just that I knew there was something."

◆

In the end, of course, I told her about Nikos Petropoulos. Once I had started it wasn't so difficult and she listened without interrupting. I was scared she would laugh it off, say I was making a fuss about nothing, that people often found themselves on different sides in a war. Even people in the same family.

When I had finished she gave a bit of a shiver and said, "It must make you feel *odd*. Why didn't someone tell you before? They must have known you'd find out one day. Why did Aunt Elena say you mustn't talk to your mother?"

"Not to upset her. You know what Mum's like."

"Aunt Bill says she ought to get married again. She needs looking after. That's the same sort of thing, I suppose. But, I don't know, I think it sounded more as if it was your *Aunt Elena* who didn't want it all talked about. Or wanted you to believe *her* story and no one else's. She's really your Great-aunt Elena, isn't she? I was muddled to start with."

"You can't go round calling people Great-aunt. Why does it matter?"

She thought and frowned, chewing on an end of her hair. Then she said slowly, "It's just so you know what age they are. Aunt Elena sounds as if she's the same age as your Uncle Emlyn. As your mother and father. But she isn't, she's more or less the same age as your grandparents."

"Okay," I said. "If Great-aunt places her better for you generation-wise, then Great-aunt it shall be."

I was feeling altogether much more cheerful. I clicked my heels together and saluted.

She gave me a vague smile. She said, "You are an ass, Plato. What I meant was, she was *there*. Your mother and father weren't even born. There's only one other person left alive in your family who was there at the time. If you want to know what really happened, you'll have to ask CLJ."

⊛CHAPTER·8

The thought of asking CLJ froze the marrow in my bones. (That isn't just something people *say*. I could actually *feel* my skeleton icing up and going creaky and stiff.)

He had always been kind to Aliki and me; when we went to stay with him he used to give us two pounds each—one pound when we arrived and one when we left. In between he smiled at us or patted our heads at mealtimes and bedtimes, and I think I can remember him reading *The Jungle Book* to me when I was young. Once. Long ago.

Aliki and I haven't been to Wales together since my father left. Now, when I go alone, CLJ gives me five pounds at the beginning and five pounds at the end. He always does this when no one is around. As if he is ashamed of giving me money. Or just doesn't want my grandmother or Uncle Emlyn to know.

I have no reason to be afraid of CLJ. And I am not exactly

afraid, anyway. Only of not being clever enough, or brave enough, or good enough for him.

This is the sort of person he is.

Years ago, when Aliki was six or seven, she had a terrible temper. No one could make her do anything she didn't want to do.

Dad was still with us then. We all lived together in a big house in Surrey. We had a huge garden with a lovely wild bit at the bottom, all trees and bluebells. Dad was working in London and Mum had someone to help her clean and cook and so she wasn't too tired and she sang as she went around the house. Sometimes CLJ came, when he had something to do in London, and sometimes he stayed several days, working upstairs in the room Mum kept ready and waiting for him. She told Aliki and me to be quiet as mice. "The poor man comes for peace," she said. (Meaning to get away from our grandmother.)

One morning Aliki decided she was not going to school. She said, "I'm not going today," and stumped up to her bedroom and slammed the door hard. In the ordinary way Mum and I would have waited until she got bored and came down, but because CLJ was upstairs in his room Mum flew after Aliki to stop her disturbing him.

It was absolutely the wrong thing to do. There was nothing Aliki liked better than disturbing people when she was in the mood for it. She threw herself on the floor and started to thump her feet up and down and scream at the top of her voice, "I won't, I won't, I won't go to school. I hate school, I hate my teacher, I hate my best friend, I hate everyone, they're all pigs, I don't want to learn anything, I don't *need* to learn anything."

At least, I *think* that is what she was saying. It came out in a great fuddled roar like someone shouting through a megaphone in a high wind. And Mum was saying, "Aliki, darling, all right, it's all right, you don't have to go to school if you're feeling ill, oh, you must be feeling so ill my precious to make all this dreadful fuss, please stop it my angel and tell Mummy *quietly* what's wrong."

As if my bawling, purple-faced sister would listen to that kind of soft pleading nonsense! I was standing in the doorway by now and I saw the cold steely look in her eyes. She had stopped roaring, but only because she was gathering her breath to roar louder.

Then CLJ was there. He said, "Come."

That was all. Just one word. Aliki turned her head to look at him. He held out his hand and she stood up and took it. CLJ nodded at me before they both set off down the stairs and I followed them.

We went out of the front door. I expected Aliki to break away and to bite his hand or kick his shins if he tried to hold on to her.

I remember feeling a bit sorry for him. Aliki had sharp teeth and she was a strong kicker.

She didn't bite or kick. She walked beside CLJ, through the garden, out of the gate, down the road. I thought she would probably try to escape when we turned the next corner. There was a side alley with a hedge on one side that fenced it off from the park. The gaps in the hedge were big enough for her to wriggle through but too small for a grown-up.

I hoped she would get away. She was a pest. I was on her side all the same.

But she just walked on, past the side alley, through the

[93]

main street, across the pedestrian crossing, all the time holding CLJ's hand very calmly and quietly—as if it had never
once crossed her mind, not even for the most minuscule
second, to throw a tantrum over going to school. When they
got to the gates, CLJ dropped her hand and gave her shoulder
a little push to send her on her way. Then he turned round
without waiting to see if she went into the playground and,
as he went past me, nodded again.

He didn't smile. That tells you something about him. Any
other grown-up who had made Aliki do something she didn't
want to do would have smirked at me. *Look how clever, how
powerful I am!* If he had smiled, I would have hated him
forever.

No one else could have got Aliki to school that morning.
Not in that way. My father could have picked her up and
carried her and thrown her in the car and put the child lock
on and thumped her if she went on yelling, and my mother
could have bribed her with money or sweets, but neither of
them could have taken her as CLJ did, without fuss.

It was as if he had some special power. Not like a general
in the army. More like a lion tamer. A people tamer. An
Aliki tamer.

I think it was then that I started to see him as different
from other grown-ups. Set apart. I wasn't frightened of him.
It was just that the thought of asking him something important made me feel cold.

◆

I wouldn't be seeing him for a while, anyway. I was going
to stay in Wales for part of the Easter holidays but there

was the rest of the term to be got through before that. And now we were living in this poky flat, there was no room for CLJ to come and stay even if he wanted to.

So that was that. I went back to school and my mother went back to work. She had changed since the funeral. She had absolutely stopped drinking gin. (I kept a strict eye on the bottle.) She started singing in the bath again. She went up to London and bought a beautiful dress of red silk and a pair of red shoes with high heels. She put on the dress on and twirled around to show me. She looked as she used to look when she and my father went out in the evenings.

I was glad she had found something to cheer her sad life. I said the dress was very pretty and her hair looked nice too. I said, "You ought to be going out to a party," and then wished I hadn't spoken. None of the people we knew nowadays were the sort to give parties and it seemed cruel to remind her.

She said, "I'm going out to dinner, that's enough of a party for an old lady like me. Tasso is in London, he's driving out to fetch me, he should be here any minute."

I didn't say anything. What was I supposed to do? Dance for joy?

She said in a coaxing voice, "You don't mind, do you, darling? You have homework to do, you don't need me here, do you?"

◆

I said to Jane, "He's here *all the time*. Well, most evenings, anyway. He has an office in London and an office in Athens and one somewhere in Switzerland and he says he can work anywhere now because of computers and faxes. So I suppose we'll never get rid of him."

"Your mother doesn't want to get rid of him, does she?" Jane said. "I think he's nice. Even if he wasn't I'd put up with it to go out in that car."

Jane had only met him once. I thought, *Women! Always taken in by appearances.*

I said, through gritted teeth, "That's only the Jaguar. He keeps an English car in England. He has a Mercedes in Greece. I expect he has a Cadillac in America. And people to drive them everywhere. Chauffeurs."

Jane sighed and rolled her eyes. She said, "He's the first really rich person I've met. Where does he get all his money?"

"Baubles," I said. "Trinkets. Gewgaws. Gold and silver. Pretty things for brainless women."

"Mmmm," Jane said. "I know something you don't. Jewelry is just a sideline. His family are the ship owners. I mean, *the* ship owners. I thought I'd seen the name in the newspaper. So I checked with Aunt Bill."

"Oh, I knew that," I lied.

I could have known it, I told myself. My mother was desperate to talk to me about Tasso—how I felt about him, whether I *minded,* that sort of thing. I just didn't want to know. He was all right as far as I could see—more than all right in the paying-of-bills and buying-pretty-dresses department—but that was as far as I was willing to go. I just wasn't interested. Or hadn't been interested. Now, suddenly, I was interested all right. And scared stiff.

I said, "You can't trust really rich people. I mean, if he'd made his own money, that's one thing. But if you're born rich, if you've always had what you wanted, new toys and things, and new cars . . ."

Jane's eyes were wide with amazement. "Your mother's not a toy," she said. "Or a car."

"Exactly," I said. "Toys and cars don't have feelings."

◆

It's all right for Jane. Her mother is dead and quite safe: no feelings to hurt any longer.

While Tasso was around, my mother was happy. Even when he wasn't in London, when he was in Geneva, or Athens, or seeing *his* old mother in Iria, she was happy because he was coming back. Or she *thought* he was coming back.

When he was out of England, he telephoned every evening, usually about nine o'clock, just before the BBC news. Mum would start to get twitchy about half an hour before. Couldn't sit still, went to the bathroom, combed her hair, sighed, put the kettle on. It wasn't the right atmosphere for a person trying to write an essay on the American Civil War, which was my special history project this term. Especially as I kept wondering if she was jumpy because at the back of her mind she was afraid he wasn't going to phone after all. Not this evening, not tomorrow, not ever again.

One evening when the phone rang at nine, it wasn't Tasso. Since she left the door to the hall open, I can give you my mother's side of the conversation.

"Oh, it's *you*. . . . No, not at all, I was expecting someone else to ring. . . . Yes, Plato's all right, doing his homework. How is Aliki? . . . Oh, good. Good."

She looked at me through the open door, smiling, eyes

[97]

shining. Quite different from her usual down-at-heel look when she talked to my father. She mouthed at me, "Do you want to speak to Dad?" I shook my head but I don't think she saw me. She had turned back to the telephone. I went back to my essay. But I kept my ears open.

"Yes. . . . Yes. . . . Yes, of course I will be happy for Aliki to come to Greece in the summer. Plato and I much look forward to seeing her. . . . But I had thought you wanted Plato to come to America . . . ? Oh. Oh, I see. Yes, I can see that would be inconvenient."

Something in her voice made me look at her. Her face looked puffy and pink suddenly, and she was chewing her bottom lip.

"So it'll be born in July? How does Aliki feel about it? . . . Oh, me, well, it doesn't make any difference to me, how could it possibly make any difference to me?"

That was most of it. There were some polite and mean-ingless phrases, on both sides presumably, hoping each other was well. Then she put the telephone down and came into the living room, hugging herself, wide-eyed and laughing.

She said, "You heard that, I expect. You are to have a new half brother or sister. So you are let off. You don't have to go to New York in the summer."

"I wasn't going anyway," I said. "I said I wouldn't go. I told you."

This was something I had been prepared to make a real fight about.

She said soothingly, "I knew that. But your father didn't. I am glad I don't have to tell him!"

The telephone rang again and she ran to answer it. This

time she said happily, breathlessly, "Oh, Tasso . . ." And closed the door.

◆

February blew itself out, then March, then it was April and coming up to Easter, and it began to seem as if I had been wrong about Tasso. He hadn't got bored with my mother and traded her in for a newer model. In fact, incredibly, he seemed even more potty about her than he had been to begin with. And having this doting person around was definitely good for her. She stopped smoking so much and said she was soon going to give it up altogether. She started to cook proper meals again. When I got back from school she was either busy in the kitchen or settled comfortably in the living room actually *reading a book!* Instead of lying in front of the telly with a glass of gin!

So I got to like Tasso a bit, for her sake. And another little bit for myself. He was sensible, he didn't try to bribe me with presents; the only thing he gave me was a marvelous Mont Blanc fountain pen, which was all right because it wasn't the sort of thing you would give to a child.

My mother said, in one of her silly voices, "That's a very special pen, Plato, you must take very great care of it."

I gave her a cold look. She ignored it, or, to be more exact, didn't see it; she was gazing at Tasso with a soppy expression. He said, "I think your son understands what is a good pen, Maria. Although it is what he will write with it that is of true value."

He was looking at me gravely, without smiling, and I knew I could trust him to take my side if he had to.

[99]

I said, "I'll try to be worthy of it," making a joke but half meaning it, too, and Tasso did smile then, gold tooth sparkling, as if he had understood perfectly.

◆

End of term, and I was going to Wales. Tasso picked us up in the Jaguar and I assumed we were going to Paddington Station, where Mum would insist on seeing me into the train and reminding me to change at Cardiff as if I were a five-year-old or a half-wit. (Not that I have anything *against* half-wits or five-year-olds, just that I wish my mother would try to remember that I am neither.)

At the end of the street the Jag turned right instead of left toward the London road, and I wondered if Tasso had made a mistake. I thought, *He must know the way*, he had come and gone often enough. But then, at the roundabout, he took the turn for the motorway.

My mother turned round to me. She said, "Surprise for you, darling. Tasso is driving us all the way. Well, not *quite* all the way. We are meeting CLJ in Cardiff for lunch and he'll take you on afterward."

Just like that! I was winded. Flabbergasted. Dumbstruck. *My mother* meeting CLJ! Not that she had ever said anything against *him*; it was my Welsh grandmother who was the fly in the ointment. Or the witch in the closet. But my Welsh grandmother was CLJ's wife. And my mother was the daughter of the treacherous Greek who had handed CLJ's life to the Germans! Offered it up as a bargaining counter. Surely Tasso must know that? He and my mother had grown up together. Gone to school together.

Like me and Jane Tucker. And I knew everything about Jane. I was fairly sure I did, anyway.

Tasso was watching me in the rearview mirror. He said, "CLJ has been a hero all my life, Plato. I have waited a long time to make his acquaintance. He and my father fought together for Greece."

I made myself smile at him. It wasn't his fault. He had asked my mother to fix this meeting and she hadn't liked to tell him that she was no longer on speaking terms with her ex-husband's family. Too proud? Or too stupid? Bit of both, probably.

On the other hand, CLJ had *agreed* to come, hadn't he?

I decided—not for the first time in what was beginning to feel quite a long life already—that once people got old, say over about nineteen or twenty, their powers of logical thinking diminished quite rapidly.

◆

Or maybe they simply get more hypocritical! When we got there—*there* being a posh country hotel several miles outside Cardiff—CLJ had just parked his antediluvian Morris Minor between a Rolls Royce and a Bentley. The moment we came to a stop my mother was out of the car and tottering toward him on her high heels and waving, and he took the pipe out of his mouth to kiss her. Then he walked toward Tasso and me with his arm round her shoulders.

He patted me on the head and said, "Grown a bit, haven't you?"

He held out both hands to Tasso, and although they didn't actually kiss each other (CLJ had his pipe back in his mouth by this time) they held each other and thumped each other like a pair of Greeks instead of one Greek and one Welshman.

And they spoke Greek as well. First Tasso and CLJ and then Mum joining in. Faster and faster and louder and louder until they were shouting as Greeks always do, sounding to foreigners as if they are quarreling. CLJ was as fast and as loud as the others, waving his hands about, laughing. I was so amazed, I could feel my jaw drop as I stared at him.

He noticed me suddenly. He said, "Tasso's father and I are the best of old friends. You must forgive us if Tasso and I speak Greek together. It is a rare pleasure for me nowadays."

Speaking English, he was CLJ again: very polite, a little stiff. High up and a long way away. Like on top of a mountain.

I said, "I don't mind."

I could have enlarged on this gracious statement. I could have said I was only too happy to sit at a table and stuff my face without having to endure the usual adult-to-child chit-chat on this sort of occasion. *How are you doing at school, little man? Very well, thank you, Grandfather.*

But CLJ had gone back to being Greek again without waiting for my kind permission. And Greek he stayed, all through what I must admit was a super-glorious lunch. (Salmon and peas and potatoes and chocolate eclairs with ice cream.) No one took any notice of me except to pass extra vegetables and, in the case of my mother, a good share of her ice cream, and I found the time passed very comfortably.

The others seemed to enjoy themselves too, though I don't think they noticed the food. Too busy talking and laughing.

They didn't bother to lower their voices in deference to the solemn feeding habits of the silent British at the other tables. If I had been a self-conscious sort of person I would have been deeply embarrassed.

Especially at the end of the meal! CLJ had said (kindly speaking in English for my sake) that he and I must be going; we would say goodbye now, and Tasso and my mother could take their time drinking their coffee. We all stood up. My mother kissed me. Tasso flung his arms around CLJ and this time they kissed each other several times on both cheeks with loud smacking noises. And when they had disentangled themselves from this passionate embrace, my mother flung herself on CLJ's chest and burst into tears.

He patted her back. He looked helplessly at Tasso and me over her shoulder. He pulled his handkerchief out of his pocket and his pipe came out with it, and a big bunch of keys, and a packet of cough lozenges called Fisherman's Friend.

I picked them up from the floor and put them on the table. Then I decided that I urgently needed to go to the lavatory.

◆

CLJ was waiting for me at the door of the dining room. He said, "I think retreat is in order. Tasso has the situation under control. Your mother is drinking a very large brandy."

We strapped ourselves into his old Morris Minor and took off. ("Took off" is right—you could feel the car gathering itself up for this great adventure like an airplane on the runway.)

I said, "My friend, Jane Tucker, her aunts have a car even older than yours. It's called Rattlebones."

"Your grandmother has named this one Boneshaker. Just as original." He puffed on his pipe; through the clouds of blue smoke I saw him smile faintly and wondered if he had been making a joke. He went on, "Your grandmother believes I have picked you up from Cardiff railway station. She may ask if you had a pleasant journey. It is entirely up to you how you answer."

I said, "If she just says, pleasant journey, I can say yes. If she says pleasant journey *by train*, that's more difficult."

I had never teased CLJ before. I wasn't sure if he had got the point. I said, "I mean, I might have to *lie.*"

He laughed so hard that he had to take his hand off the steering wheel to catch his pipe before it fell into his lap, almost losing control of the ancient vehicle. We nearly went into the ditch. Safely back on the road, he said, "I think, Plato, that to answer no more than *yes* to the first question would be to lie by implication. That is—"

"I *know.*" I couldn't help showing off. "You mean, *normally,* I would say yes, it was a nice, clean train, or, we were half an hour late leaving Paddington but we made up time later. Just to say yes by itself when I know she's really asking about what it was like on the train is a kind of cheating. Unless I *had* come by train, of course!"

CLJ was chuckling now, hanging onto his pipestem with his long, brown-stained teeth. "I think I can leave you to work it out for yourself," he said.

He was silent after that for ten minutes. I know it was ten minutes because I kept looking at my watch and wondering if I dared ask him about Nikos Petropoulos. My mouth went dry. What did I want to ask, anyway?

When the ten minutes were up CLJ wound down the

window, took his pipe out of his mouth, and banged it on the outside of his door. Then he closed the window, put the pipe on the dashboard, and took a Fisherman's Friend out of his pocket.

He cleared his throat. "I was glad to see Maria so happy. That was a bad business."

I supposed he meant my father clearing off with the Dentist-Doll. I wondered if he knew about the new baby.

But that seemed to be all he was going to say on that topic. He sucked on his Fisherman's Friend. We had climbed up out of a valley and were crossing the top of the mountain: cropped green grass and sheep bleating and lots of newborn lambs staggering after their mothers. Another five minutes passed.

CLJ said, "I was sorry to hear about your other grand-father, Plato. He was a good man."

Silence again. I wasn't timing him now. I had jammed my wrists between my knees to stop my hands shaking, and my heart—or something very like it, a kind of throbbing *lump*—had climbed up into my throat.

CLJ said, "Tasso telephoned me the day before yesterday. He told me he had talked to Elena. I should have told you myself about Nikos and me. I see that now. Very remiss of me."

I was watching the baby lambs. There was one little black one suckling its mother, its tail waggling wildly. I thought, *The black sheep.*

"My friend Nikos was a brave man," CLJ said firmly. "He had an impossible decision to make. Between honor and death and dishonor and life."

He looked at me in a questioning way, rather as if he

wasn't sure I was capable of understanding what he had to tell me. In fact, to tell the truth, I didn't quite understand what he had just said, but I did my best to look intelligent, which is not easy when you have to wear thick glasses that make your eyes look huge and swimmy. Like watery poached eggs.

CLJ made a clicking noise with his teeth and turned back to the road. He said, "Not his own life and death, that would have been easy. Nikos had a harder choice to make. He chose dishonor and life. To save the people in his village he had to sacrifice his honor. He had to go crawling to the Germans like a peddler, trading the useful lives of Greek soldiers for the useless lives of old men and little boys who were too old or too young to fight. That's why few Greek men will forgive him. He didn't just betray his friends and his brothers in the mountains, he betrayed his country. In their view."

I swallowed. I said, "What do you think?"

"Now? Now I think what I've told you. That he was a brave man. I am not sure that in his place I would have had the courage to do what he did."

I thought, *Well, he would say that* to me, *wouldn't he?*

"Okay," I said. "What did you feel *then*?"

CLJ picked up his empty pipe and sucked on the stem. Like a baby with a dummy. Then he said, "I'm not sure I can remember. I was too busy trying to stay alive to think about moral issues."

I didn't say anything. I waited. I thought, *He can't dodge it. Won't try.* Not many people are absolutely and always honest but CLJ is one of them.

At last he said, "In a decent society the young and strong

protect the weak. You take care of children because they are the future and you take care of the old because they took care of you when you were young. A fair return."

He stopped the car in a farm gateway, took his tobacco tin out of his pocket, and began to fill his pipe. He said, "That's in peacetime. A war changes things. There are different priorities. An old man is just another mouth to feed and the children are only the future if there is going to be a future. But a young man is a gun."

I said, "You mean Nikos should have let all those people be *murdered* because they couldn't fight? And let the village burn? That's *horrible*."

CLJ was lighting his pipe. A loose shred of tobacco flared and crackled. Bitter black smoke filled the car. He flapped it away with his hand and coughed.

"The Germans might have hanged them anyway. And burned the village. They were lucky to have an unusually softhearted and decent commandant. That wasn't my point, though."

He looked at me, wiry eyebrows drawn together, wondering how best to explain his meaning to my infant mind.

I said, "Winning the war was the most important thing. So Nikos should never have said where the guerrillas were? Is that what you thought?"

"No. Not even then. I don't think I *thought* at all to begin with. I just ran for my life. But it was what my friends in the mountains believed. What most of the village will have gone on believing. That Nikos betrayed the soldiers who were fighting for Greece and shamed them all in the eyes of their country."

I thought of the men of the village standing silent as the coffin passed. I said, "If it weren't for him, some of them wouldn't be alive to despise him. It's not *fair*."

CLJ said, "Another man would have left his village. Nikos didn't see why he should be driven away. He had done what he thought was the right thing to do. So by staying put he was defending *his* honor in the only way he knew how. Elena understood that, so did her sister, your Greek grandmother." He grinned at me suddenly and started the engine. "Not your other grandmother, unfortunately."

"She was upset because you might have been shot."

"Not only that. It's her nature. I'm a peaceable type, she's the fighter. The warrior. She'd bomb women and children if that's what it took to win."

He put the car into gear and swung out of the gateway without looking in the offside mirror to see if the road was clear. He was usually a cautious driver. But his mind was elsewhere.

"We won't mention this conversation to your grandmother, Plato."

"No, sir."

He nodded appreciatively. "Good boy."

He wound down the window and banged out his pipe again and got another Fisherman's Friend out of his pocket. Then he asked me how Aliki was, and how I was doing at school, and after that, nothing more. I had the feeling that this was the longest conversation I would ever have with him. He had said all he had to say; now he was going to leave me to "work it out" for myself.

He said one more thing. We came over the last mountain and saw the valley beneath us, the rows of terrace houses climbing the hillside, and the black, deserted machinery of the old coal mine.

"You're a lucky lad, having two countries where you are at home," he said. "Where you belong. When you go back, give my love to Elena."

⊛CHAPTER · 9

Going back to Iria was too far away to bear thinking about. Over two months. But apart from the two weeks' penal sentence in the custody of my Welsh grandmother, May and June passed with tolerable speed. Nothing particular happened to make time go faster; it was just the same old things happening over and over. In their different, and separate, boxes. School Life. Home Life. Private (Secret and Thinking) Life.

◆

School Life. Nothing much to report there. At the beginning of the summer term we had to choose next year's subjects and I decided to take Ancient Greek. Owing to the weird and incomprehensible way our school curriculum is devised, this meant giving up physics. I went to the headmaster. He said, "I'm afraid we can't rearrange everything for your benefit, Plato."

It gave him great pleasure to say this. Our headmaster is against education. I think he thinks it isn't healthy. Anyone who says he wants to learn must have something wrong with him.

◆

Home Life. Tasso phoned in the mornings as well as the evenings. My mother was immensely cheerful, chirping away like a happy sparrow all day and out every night whenever Tasso was in London: dancing, eating, going to the theater. Luckily Aunt Sophie had sprained a wrist and couldn't play the drums, so she was at home, doing the cooking for Jane and Aunt Bill, and was kind enough to invite me to supper most evenings. So I didn't starve. In fact, quite the opposite. And yet, it was curious, I always seemed to be hungry.

"More potatoes, Plato? Can you manage another piece of rabbit pie?"

You bet I could! When Jane and I cleared away afterward I scraped every plate, every dish, every last shred of meat, mopping up the last drop of gravy with a crust of bread.

Jane said, "Sure you wouldn't like a sandwich to eat on the way home? It must take you all of fifteen minutes on the bike. Too long to go without food, you might faint from hunger."

"Don't torment the boy, Jane," Aunt Bill said.

But Jane wasn't so wide of the mark. If not exactly fainting, I was usually ready for a savory morsel when I got back to the flat. Luckily my mother had not altogether forsaken her maternal duties and there was always something in the fridge that could be squashed between slices of bread to keep my stomach from complaining during the night; my favorite tidbit was cold cooked butcher's sausages with plenty of mustard. Although I used to hate milk I had taken to it recently as if I were a young calf; a liter at a time would go down without touching the tonsils.

When I wasn't in fact eating or drinking I was thinking about eating and drinking. I even looked forward to the school midday dinner, which I had assumed until now was something only a famine victim could fancy.

◆

I dreamed about food. It spilled out of my Home Life into the third compartment: my Private (or Secret) Life.

I dreamed that I was at a feast in a castle in the Middle Ages and there was a roasted boar's head with an orange in its mouth on the table in front of me and woke up famished, my stomach *flapping*. I had three fried eggs and six slices of bacon that morning for breakfast and two huge bowls of Coco-pops after, and several thick slices of toast.

"Didn't you have anything to eat last night, Plato?" my mother said. "I'm sure I left something in the fridge for you."

She had. Half a cold chicken and coleslaw. I had eaten it with a large tin of baked beans. And I had had one of Aunt Sophie's suppers beforehand.

I said, "I expect I'm eating because I'm unhappy, don't you? That's usually why people eat too much. It's a kind of compensation."

I thought it was time she had something to worry about. Being so happy with Tasso was getting her out of the habit!

But perhaps there was some truth in it, too. I was still churned up in my mind about Nikos Petropoulos. Not because I was ashamed of him any longer but because I was on his side.

This was partly something I had worked out for myself and partly something Uncle Emlyn had said.

◆

He had been away when I went to stay with CLJ and my grandmother, taking a party of boys from his school on a special mathematics course in North Wales—*Extra math! In the holidays?* My headmaster would have been outraged!—but he was back for the last couple of days, and we went for one of our walks on the mountain.

I told him what Aunt Elena had said about CLJ being part of me, which meant Nikos Petropoulos was part of me too. The Coward and the Hero. I said, making a joke of it, so he wouldn't think I took it too seriously, "It's like having two people inside me who don't get on with each other. I mean, they might start a war any minute!"

He didn't even smile. He stopped walking to get his breath and stood in the wind, white hair blowing, and looked at me very seriously. He said, "That's a stupid trap to fall into. Pinning labels on people."

He sounded angry. Although I didn't think he was angry with me. He said, "Easy enough to be a hero if you're shut away from everyday life, living in a cave with a pack of young men all set for death or glory. But your Greek grandfather was living with ordinary people in the village where he'd been born. There were old men who'd been young when he was a lad, and their grandsons he had watched growing from babies. Would you call Nikos a hero if he had allowed those old men and little boys to be hanged from the tree in the square? You think on that, laddie! Put CLJ in Nikos's place if it helps you to think a bit straighter! Ask yourself what you'd say about CLJ if he'd kept his mouth shut and let them all die!"

Uncle Emlyn was so excited, spit flew from his mouth. He shouted, "You wouldn't have called him a hero, I tell you! You'd have called him a murderer!"

He glared at me. Then, suddenly, the blood came up in his face until his skin turned practically purple. He took a deep, wheezing breath, muttered something about getting home before the rain came—although there was barely a cloud in the sky—and turned on his heel.

I followed him home. I was quite stunned. I had thought Uncle Emlyn loved and admired CLJ. But he had sounded, just then, as if he was closer to hating him.

It couldn't be true, of course. You couldn't really hate someone like CLJ. Even if Uncle Emlyn got fed up sometimes with the way CLJ hogged the limelight, he couldn't really be jealous of his own father. It wasn't as if CLJ was a boastful or bumptious person.

I puzzled over this but not very hard. I was suddenly feeling too hungry for philosophical speculation. All I could think about was whether my grandmother would make us drop scones for tea—those little, light pancakes that are cooked on a griddle and eaten with lashings of salty Welsh butter. There is nothing like a plate of drop scones for hunger.

Uncle Emlyn shares my opinion, except that he prefers his butter unsalted because he likes to eat blueberry jelly as well and salty butter fights with the sweetness. One good thing I can say about my grandmother is that she respects important likes and dislikes of this kind; she always puts both kinds of butter on the table in two separate dishes.

This particular afternoon the salt butter was especially good. It was yellow as a cowslip and covered with beads of water, as good Welsh butter should be. "I went to Owen's farm up the mountain," my grandmother said, as she put a huge plate of drop scones on the table between me and Uncle Emlyn. "Just to tempt Plato's appetite."

Since it could hardly have escaped her notice that I had been falling on my food like a starving tiger, this remark was meant as a joke. Not that you would have guessed it from my grandmother's expression, which was as fierce and tight-lipped as usual. I said, "Well, you've certainly led *me* into temptation," and helped myself to a hefty slash of the sweating gold glory, glancing at her to see if she had caught the biblical reference.

She said automatically, "Don't mock the Scriptures, Plato. And remember, greed is a sin. A good appetite is one thing, eating people out of house and home quite another."

I bowed my head meekly and exchanged a sly look with Uncle Emlyn, who was demolishing his first stack of drop scones dripping with creamy pale unsalted butter and heaped with dark purple jelly. He was his ordinary self again, stuffing his face, talking to CLJ (who was also eating drop scones but rather less lustily) about the latest football scores, about some letter they'd both read in *The Times* about Cyprus, and about Uncle Emlyn's jaunt to North Wales with his mathematical prodigies.

Uncle Emlyn didn't even sound fretful, let alone angry. But from that day onward I began to see him as a sad person.

◆

Perhaps it was only the kind of general despair about life and the state of the world that is supposed to afflict people in adolescence—psychological growing pains—but I seemed to be at a stage of feeling sorry for just about everyone.

I was sorry for Uncle Emlyn. I was sorry for CLJ because he had to live with my grandmother and because the most interesting part of his life was behind him. I was sorry for my mother because she was so happy and that seemed to me dangerous. I was sorry for Great-aunt Elena because she had fallen in love with CLJ when she was fifteen and never loved anyone since. (I couldn't be sure of this but the gloomy mood I was in, it seemed likely.)

But most of all I was sorry for Nikos Petropoulos. And more than just sorry. When I thought over what Uncle Emlyn had said about how unfair it was that he should be labeled a coward, I got a burning pain in my stomach. Just to think of the way his village had treated him made me feel sick inside.

Knowing we would have to go to Molo when we went to Greece in the summer, to help my mother clear out her father's house, didn't exactly make me feel easier.

Jane said, "The people in the village can't have it in for you all that much, can they? I mean, everyone knows about CLJ, and you're *his* grandson, too. That might not have counted for much at the *funeral* because you were part of your Greek family then."

I tried to explain. "I don't care about that, not much anyway. It's just, I *hate* all these people for being so unfair to him! I mean, he saved their *lives*, some of them, anyway, and it's so sort of *righteous* and *smug*. . . . I don't know . . . I just want to *tell* them . . ."

"Put them right? I bet you have arguments with them in your head."

"Don't laugh," I said.

"I'm not laughing."

We were sitting on the wall at the bottom of Jane's garden. We had had supper and it was time I went home, but it was a lovely warm evening. Late June. Mum and I were flying off in a fortnight and Aliki would be there before us, staying with Aunt Elena.

Jane said, "If I could speak Greek I could help you explain to them just how unfair they were to your grandfather."

"Pigs might fly," I said automatically. Then I saw the look on her face.

She said, "You ought to know. Your mum asked Aunt Bill if I'd like to come with you. I think it's meant as a sort of thank-you for the way we've been feeding her ravening monster son. It's supposed to be a surprise, but I thought you ought to be warned. So you can say no."

◆

Well. It did present a bit of a problem. Naturally I wanted Jane to come. She was my best friend. (Not my *girl* friend, as my mother insisted on calling her in spite of my protests, just my best *friend*.) But although I said all the right things, grinning with delight until my jaw started cracking, secretly—so deeply inside of me that even Jane couldn't have guessed them—unworthy thoughts began to creep in.

Jane would want to go swimming. She is older than I am and she looks older still. And the beaches in Greece are full of young men with huge bulging muscles and gleaming brown skin and faces like ancient gods. And because Greek families keep a close watch on their daughters, their sons chase the foreign girls all the summer.

"You'd think their families would stop them," I said to my mother, having brought the conversation round to this aspect of Greek male behavior and hoping it would make her aware of the danger Jane would be in if she came with us. Not, to be honest, that I wanted my mother to take back her invitation. I wanted Jane to come with us.

My mother said, "Perhaps the Greek mothers and fathers like to think that their sons are getting free tuition in a foreign language."

I thought this was a flippant remark and said so, fairly sharply.

She looked at me absently as if she hadn't heard. She said, "You know, you're going to need some new clothes. You've grown so much, nothing fits you."

◆

I suppose I must have known, really. Getting dressed had become a bit of a struggle. But I had given up measuring myself. I hadn't made any marks on the back of my door for over a year now. And I had always avoided looking at myself. Other people had to put up with my disgusting appearance. I didn't see why I should suffer unnecessarily.

As the song says, "My face I don't mind it because I'm behind it, It's others in front get the view."

I hated going to buy clothes. Having to go to the children's department was bad enough. Being forced to gaze at my scrawny form in the long mirrors in the changing room was a kind of humiliation I wouldn't wish on my worst enemy.

I said, "I won't want anything in Greece except old shorts and jeans."

"What old shorts? What old jeans? Look at you! Nothing fastens!"

I begged her, "Can't you let them out? Put extra bits in? It's a waste of money."

But my mother was in a mood to spend money, it seemed. She took me to London, to Kensington, and marched me into a smart-looking Italian chain store where all the assistants wore big, floppy silk shirts and lots of junky gold jewelry. Bracelets and earrings.

"We can't afford this sort of place," I hissed at her.

What I was really afraid of was that one of those silk-shirted men would look down his nose at me and say something like, "I'm afraid we don't cater for little boys, madam."

Instead, the person who came to help us looked me up and down and said, "You're about my height, I'd say, perhaps a bit broader across the shoulders . . ."

And swept a lot of stuff off the rails.

I followed him to the cubicle numb with amazement. He didn't look all that short to me! Just medium, I would have said. I wondered if there was some kind of faulty connection between his eye and his brain.

In the cubicle mirror our shoulders were on a level and, as he had said, mine were broader. Though since I didn't look any different to myself, this simply dwindled *him* in my eyes. He was merely a midget like me!

After all, if I had really grown all that much, looked as *elderly* as I did in that mirror, someone would have said something.

I got into a pair of narrow yellow jeans and a pink shirt with big sleeves. To my surprise, the effect was not totally awful. I took my hideous glasses off but as you might expect I couldn't see what I looked like without them, so I put them back on again and strode boldly out of the cubicle to peacock in front of my mother. Waiting for her to say something.

All she said was, "Very nice, *I* think. Do you?"

I said, "Hardly the sort of gear to climb mountains in."

"We'll go to M and S later. This place is for fun!" She grinned at me, her eyes lighting up. "Give those macho Greek boys a taste of competition!"

We bought the yellow jeans and the pink shirt and another pair of pants and a couple more shirts that were not quite so fancy but just as expensive. Then we went to Marks and Spencer, which was less exciting but where I felt more at home, and spent some more money.

Tasso's money, I assumed. "Can he afford it?" I wondered out loud.

"What?" She looked put out for a minute. Then she laughed, and blushed.

I said, "I suppose I was getting to look a bit like a scarecrow, arms and legs sticking out."

That was a pretty strong hint, I thought. But still she said nothing.

Nor did anyone else. I put on the fancy gear when I went to supper with Jane, and she said nothing, nor did Aunt Bill or Aunt Sophie. The aunts admired the clothes but did not mention the other, more important matter.

I began to think it must be all in my mind. There was one way to check, of course, and I must admit that half a dozen times I was tempted. But I was afraid. Just the thought of standing with my back against the door and a ruler on my head, measuring myself against those scratchy old marks, made me sweat. I had decided over a year ago to abandon that particular torture. There was no point in starting it up again.

I refused to think about it. I refused to talk about it. I refused to look at myself in the mirror. It didn't *matter!* Whether I was short and stumpy or tall and thin, I was still *me!*

◆

Aunt Bill drove us to Heathrow. Rattlebones was rattling so much that I began to think she would fall apart on the motorway. Though if she had done, we could probably have mended her with a screwdriver and a piece of string.

But she got us there, and we said goodbye to Aunt Bill and hung about for hours, the way you do at airports nowadays. Jane had never flown before so the whole boring routine was more interesting to her than it was to my mother and me; by the time we got on the plane she was still bright and excited instead of stupid and stunned with the tedium. She even thought the miserably cramped seats were comfortable! (If Tasso had had his way we would have been flying first class, but although my mother was pleased to accept dinners and theaters and clothes for her son, airplane tickets were off limits, apparently.)

My mother had the window seat, I had the aisle seat, and Jane sat between us. She rummaged in the pocket in front of her. "Magazines," she said. "There's a menu card and a list of duty-free things . . ."

"And a sick bag," I said.

She looked at me. "Why are you so grouchy? Grouching about having to wait, grouching about the seats."

"There's no room. They keep cramming in more and more seats. If they go on like this, the only people able to fly in an airplane will be legless dwarfs!"

Jane said, "I'm all right and I'm not a dwarf. You've just grown too tall. You shouldn't have eaten so much if your object in life was to stay the right size for an airplane seat."

I stared at her.

She put her hand to her mouth, pretending to be shocked. "Oh, I'm *sorry*," she said. "I shouldn't have mentioned it. I promised Aunt Sophie."

I started to laugh. I was drinking fizzy lemonade and it went down the wrong way. I went on laughing all the time I was snorting and choking and Jane thumped me on the back and I could hear my mother's anxious-hen cluckings from the far side of her.

When I could speak, I gasped, "Why didn't you tell me *before?* I thought I'd gone mad."

Both my mother and Jane were laughing now. Jane said, "We thought you'd be insulted. As if we hadn't liked you as you used to be. There's no personal credit in growing, it's something everyone does, so why mention it? That's what you'd say, we thought. That sort of thing, anyway."

So they had all been discussing me, had they? My terrible

sensitivity on this subject. *Poor Plato, he minds so much about being a weed, we mustn't upset him!*

I could have objected. Instead, I said cheerfully, "And here was me thinking I was suffering from delusions. I mean, I *looked* taller, I *felt* taller, but no one else seemed to notice. What d'you think that does, eh? A sensitive person like me might have been driven quite loopy!"

The seat felt comfortable suddenly. The sky around us was pale and clear. Soft white clouds rolled and billowed beneath us. They would bring us lunch in a minute, fastening trays across us as if we were babies in high chairs. In another two and a half hours or so we would be in Athens. Tasso would meet us. I would be pleased to see Tasso but there was someone else I would be more pleased to see. In fact, couldn't wait to see.

I leaned across Jane. I said, "I say, Mum, d'you know if Tasso is going to bring Aliki to meet us?"

CHAPTER · 10

But Aliki wasn't at Athens to meet us. She'd had a bad cold when she arrived from New York, Tasso said, and Aunt Elena had kept her in bed.

If Tasso made no comment on my changed appearance, it was not out of tender concern for my feelings. He didn't take a proper look at either Jane or me. He greeted us loudly and energetically, kissing Jane noisily on both cheeks and thumping me so hard between the shoulder blades that I was almost knocked breathless, but he only really *looked* at my mother.

I couldn't measure myself against Aliki-the-Giantess and Tasso was too occupied gazing into my mother's eyes to pay me any attention. So I was stuck with Jane. I said, "I'm taller than you."

She was busy looking around her—Athens airport was her first sight of a foreign country. She said impatiently,

"So? You've been taller for quite a while. You never were all that much shorter anyway. Does it matter?"

"No. But it only doesn't matter in the way people say money doesn't matter when they've got a lot of it. What d'you mean, I never was all that much shorter?"

"Just that you weren't. Aunt Bill said . . ." She stopped. "Oh, it's too *boring!*"

"Not to me. What did Aunt Bill say?"

She sighed. "Just that it was all to do with your dad going off and feeling you ought to look after your mother. That you were trying to grow up too fast and it meant you hated falling behind. Even when it was something you couldn't do anything about." She hesitated, looking at me as if wondering what to say next. Then she went on, in a rush, "Aunt Bill said it wasn't surprising you had a few hangups. She said you were—oh, I don't remember exactly. Something soppy, like 'a gallant young person.' "

She snorted and giggled, red with embarrassment.

I was embarrassed, too. I said, "Your Aunt Bill! The only person I know who talks to plants and motorcars as if they were people!"

Which had nothing to do with what Jane had told me, of course.

Outside the airport the heat struck like a hand. Although Tasso's Mercedes was air conditioned, he drove with the windows open once he was out of Athens. "It is to feel part of the country," he said. "To sit in the cool, with closed windows, you become alien, shut away from this world. You don't mind, Maria?"

My mother said, happily, "I like the Greek air."

Jane and I went to sleep in the car. I woke up once when we stopped at a level crossing to let a train pass—Greek trains make a lot of noise, grunting and groaning and blowing their whistles. And a second time to find we were climbing a hill very slowly behind an old, rickety lorry that was loaded with huge chunks of pink and gray marble. The lorry's exhaust was belching out stinking black smoke. I wondered if I should point out to my mother that at this precise moment her favorite "Greek air" was practically pure carbon monoxide. But then Tasso swung out and accelerated past the lorry and I could smell the real Greece again: a lovely, hot, herby smell, thyme and honey, rising up from the baked land either side of the road.

The next time I woke, we were in Iria, in the square, and Aunt Elena was there, and Aliki, pale-faced and pink-nosed from her cold, suddenly bursting out crying as she ran to hug Mum. She cried more like an abandoned baby who was too young to understand that her mother had not left her forever than a girl of eleven. I felt so sad for her that I began to feel weepy myself.

I said, to Jane, "Sorry about the orgy of sentiment. Aliki always puts on this mushy act. Sometimes it's almost convincing."

Jane wasn't listening. She was looking around her, taking in everything: the little square, the old houses, the church, the bare, rocky mountain that reared up behind, crowned with the great ruined castle. The rock and the battlements were pink in the evening light.

She swung round to look at me, her eyes bright as beads. "Oh, Plato! Why didn't you tell me it was such a magical place!"

I forbore to remind her that the last time I had suggested that Iria might have some small advantages over the featureless suburb we were forced to inhabit in England, she had snapped my head off.

But she had remembered. She put her hand to her mouth and laughed. She said, "Perhaps it's more of a surprise this way, after all."

She was fizzing with happiness—as if she might suddenly rise up in the air like a rocket. When Aunt Elena came to welcome her, holding her hand out, Jane said, her voice singing, "Oh, I'm so glad to be here, it's so kind of you to let me come." And instead of shaking her hand, Aunt Elena pinched her lovingly (but very hard *indeed*) on both cheeks.

Aliki came forward shyly; when I kissed her and put my arm round her she peered past me at Jane, sucking her hair.

And I was able to *tuck her under my armpit* to introduce her.

◆

The next few days were very hot. Aliki and Elena and my mother slept after lunch but Jane was too excited for a siesta so we went to the beach. We swam and lay in the shade of the eucalyptus trees and swam again, floating in the flat, clear, warm sea and looking up at the rock and the castle. "Oh," Jane said. "*Oh!*"

Her wet hair streamed in the water like seaweed. "Have you lost the power of speech?" I said. "Or have you decided to make only grunting noises for the rest of your life?"

She didn't bother to answer. Or she didn't hear me. "Oh!" seemed all she was capable of saying. "Oh!" when we showed her the hole CLJ had been hidden in. "Oh!" when we puffed up to the top of the castle and looked from the highest tower to the little town huddled beneath it and across the sea to the long, sleeping shapes of the islands, smoky in the heat haze. "Oh!" when she saw an old lady in black riding her donkey sidesaddle and beating her feet up and down to keep the blood going. "Oh!" when we saw the Gypsy girls on the beach, running in and out of the water with all their clothes on, ducking each other and laughing, and then sitting on the rocks, their wet skirts spread out around them, glittery with spangles and sun.

I am exaggerating a little. But not all that much. For about three days, although Jane said all the polite things she had to say to everyone else and was especially nice to Aliki, she hardly spoke to me. She wasn't ignoring me; she smiled from time to time and crossed her eyes to make me laugh. I guessed she was just in a sort of happy dream, the way I was sometimes when I had read a book or seen a film that was so especially good that I needed to stay quiet afterward, to keep it whole and unspoiled for as long as I could.

"Oh!" she said at last. "Oh, Plato! I couldn't imagine anywhere so beautiful. I never want to leave, ever."

But we had to go to Molo. Had she forgotten? It had been lurking like a grim shadow at the back of my mind. Only for two or three days, my mother had said, but the sooner the better. It would be better to be higher up in this very hot weather.

I said, "I expect, if you want, you can stay here while Mum and I go to the village. It might be a good idea, actually. Mum doesn't really want to take Aliki and Aliki won't mind staying if you're staying too."

Jane pulled a magnificently horrible face, crossing her eyes until they seemed to vanish completely into the crease of her nose and widening her nostrils into huge caverns. She looked like a blind, mad troll.

"Stop it," I said, when I could speak. My ribs hurt with laughing. "Please, Jane, you'll *stick*."

She wriggled her nose and was Jane again. "Well, don't you be such a fool then! 'Course I'm coming. All I meant was, I never want to leave Iria again *in my mind*."

◆

In the end, we all went: Aunt Elena and Aliki and Jane and me. Enough work for everyone, Aunt Elena said. Tasso had wanted to come but he had to go to Athens and my mother said she was glad of it.

"This is something I have to do on my own," she said.

I was going to say that she would hardly be on her own with the four of us, but Aunt Elena gave me a look like a lightning flash and I held my tongue.

The taxi went very fast, swerving round corners and bouncing hard on the rough bits of the road. Aunt Elena and my mother hung on to each other in the front seat, next to the driver, and Aliki and Jane and I were thrown about in the back like sacks of potatoes.

We arrived during the siesta. I think my mother had thought no one would notice us at that time of day. She showed no other sign of nervousness except for looking rather more pink-cheeked and determined than usual as we got out of the taxi and lugged the stuff we'd brought with us, the food and the sleeping bags, down to the house from the path.

Inside, the house smelled of cat. There was a scuffling

sound in the attic upstairs and Aunt Elena said, "Nikos had many cats. He fed all the strays, and there are always lots of stray cats in a village. When he died, they all vanished, but it seems some may have come back."

We took the sleeping bags up to the attic which was bare boards, no furniture, and lots of bird droppings. No sign of a cat.

Aliki kicked at the bird droppings. "Ugh!" she said. "Gross! Do we have to sleep here?"

"Unless you sleep on the terrace," I said. "And if you sleep outside, wild animals might come and nibble your toes."

Aliki shivered. "Mum says there are wolves and bears up the mountain. Deep in the forest."

She looked really scared. I said, "There are bears round the lake where you go in the summer with Dad."

She said, "But those are *American* bears."

Jane and I laughed and she scowled. "I'm not going to sleep with all this bird mess. I want to sleep in a *bed*."

Well, you can't, I was going to say, but Jane shook her head, just the tinest movement. She said, "We can pretend to be hiding. Like CLJ. It'll be much nicer than that hole he was stuck in, especially when it's all swept and tidy. Do you want to help me, Aliki?"

I took the hint and went downstairs and left them to it.

The only two bedrooms in the house were on the ground floor, one leading off the tiny sitting room and the other a narrow slit of a room behind the big kitchen. This bedroom had an iron bedstead in it, a bedside table with a lamp, a big wooden chest under the small window, and bookshelves that reached to the ceiling.

Aunt Elena was taking down the books one by one, dusting them, and putting them into a cardboard box.

"This is where your grandfather slept," she said. "He never slept in the marriage bed after your grandmother died."

I looked at a few of the books. There were some English books, novels and poetry, but most were in Greek.

I said, "What was my grandmother's name?"

"Maria," Aunt Elena said. "Maria. Your mother was named after her. Nikos had a good picture of her somewhere. Better than any I have. Your mother is looking for it in the other bedroom."

This room was quite different. There were no books. The bed was big, with high wooden sides and a wooden headboard covered with carvings of birds and stiff little girls with skirts like bells and legs and arms sticking out. There were two high-backed, heavy chairs, and two tables with white lace cloths on them, and some heavy red curtains. My mother was kneeling in front of an open chest. She was holding a photograph in a silver frame.

I looked at it over her shoulder. My grandmother, Maria Petropoulos. The same name as my mother, but she looked much sterner and stronger. She was also very much fatter.

My mother had photographs of her mother at home, stuck in an album, but I had never taken much notice. She had died so long ago. My mother couldn't remember her.

Now I looked at this photograph carefully and tried to feel something about this person who was one of my ancestors. But I couldn't feel anything. I said, "It must feel funny to you, not to have known her."

My mother put her hand up and I held it over her shoulder.

She said, "It doesn't worry me, it never did. I always thought of Aunt Elena as my mother. Just now, I was thinking of my father. There seems so little of him left. Only his books." She gave a long, shuddery sigh. She said, "Oh, Plato, sometimes I wish I was a really religious person."

I thought I had better put a stop to this morbid talk. I said, "Could we take some of the books home?"

"What's the point? I don't suppose I shall read them and you can't read Greek, anyway."

"I might learn," I said. "Wonders never cease."

◆

My mother chose a carved wooden chest to send back to England, and we put some of the books into it, and a few lace cloths that she thought she might use at home, and a brass oil lamp that she said would look pretty in the hall of our flat. Aunt Elena would store the rest of the furniture, and most of the books were to go to the library in Iria.

"Now we must clean out the kitchen," Aunt Elena said. "Not something you can help with, my chickens. Run off and amuse yourselves. Go to the square. When it is time to eat I will know where to find you."

◆

This was a moment I had been dreading. It was evening, a red sun setting, and everyone was up and about. The square would be full of people watching and staring. I felt my ears start to burn as we climbed up to the path and a man stood up on the terrace of the next house and looked at us.

He was a big man with black hair with a lot of gray in it and a brown face so solidly wrinkled that it could have been

[132]

carved out of wood. I thought, *He must be old enough to remember the war. Even, perhaps, to have fought in it. Had he hated my grandfather?*

In Greece, in the country, which is anywhere outside Athens, even strangers greet each other as they pass. Good morning, good afternoon, how are you? This man, our grandfather's neighbor, just watched us.

Aliki called out, "*Kalispera.*" Good evening.

For a second, I thought he was not going to answer her. But she was standing still, waiting, and at last he said in a slow, rusty voice, "*Kalispera sas.*"

Then he swung on his heel and walked to the end of his terrace and stood with his back to us.

"You see!" I said. "He doesn't want to have anything to do with us."

"He didn't throw stones at us, anyway," Aliki said.

"I think he's just looking at the sunset," Jane said. "It's lovely. Look at that funny pink cloud!"

It wasn't like any cloud I had seen before. It seemed to be resting on top of the mountain; it was like a huge, soft, pinky orange meringue. The rest of the sky was still a clear daytime blue, no other cloud in sight anywhere. The cloud was so brightly colored it was almost as if the sun was shining behind it. But the sun was slowly sinking in another part of the sky.

"It must be some sort of reflection," Jane said.

We were on the path, walking toward the square. Jane was looking back, over her shoulder, and frowning a little. I said, "You get peculiar effects sometimes in the Aegean. It's something to do with barometric pressure. A change in the weather."

[133]

I didn't know if this was true or not but it sounded all right. And I was too worried about how people would behave to us when we got to the square to pay much attention to meteorology.

I wasn't afraid for myself. But Jane had never been in a foreign country before. And Aliki was always liable to do something stupid.

We passed a boy driving about a dozen sheep home from the mountain. I said "*Yassu,*" and he said "*Yassu*" back, grinning and waving his stick. That made me feel a bit braver.

We had fallen into single file to let the sheep pass, and I stayed ahead. Behind me I could hear Aliki telling Jane a story about a conversation between a Greek shepherd and an Australian sheep farmer. The Greek asked the Australian how many sheep he had. "Four thousand or so at the last count," the Australian said. "And how many shepherds?" the Greek shepherd asked. "Just a couple," the Australian said. "*Po, po, po,*" the Greek cried in astonishment. "How do you milk four thousand sheep with only two shepherds?"

We were at the end of the path now and the busy square was before us. Jane didn't laugh, and Aliki said, "You see, Greek shepherds *milk* their sheep but the Australian didn't understand that!"

"Yes," Jane said. "Yes, it's a very funny story, Aliki. Plato—Oh, Plato, *look* . . . Turn round and look . . ."

I didn't turn round at once. The people in the square, who had been standing in small groups and talking, or sitting at the café tables, were all suddenly staring toward me. My heart seemed to miss several beats.

Then I saw that they weren't staring at me, but at something beyond me. I turned about and saw scarlet light flaring round the edges of the strange cloud. It was a cloud of *smoke*, growing and billowing as it swept down the mountain, and there were red and yellow flames crackling and leaping behind and around it.

CHAPTER · 11

People were running and shouting. Women began to wail and tug at their hair. Other people shook their fists at the sky. And across the square, a man howled like a wolf and beat his head against a stone wall.

Aliki said, in a loud voice, "The fire's a long way away. Right over the valley."

She was scared, all the same. She came to stand close to me.

I said, "They're all olive trees there. That side of the mountain."

Aliki took hold of my hand. "Will they send water planes? Or is it too windy? The sea was rough yesterday."

Jane said, "What are water planes?"

"Don't you *know*?"

Aliki stared at her. She had been to Greece often enough to know things without knowing she knew them. Things that foreigners might not understand. Like the value of olive trees. And the terrible danger of fires.

I said, "Water planes land on the sea and scoop it up in their tanks and spray it over the fires. But they're no good in rough weather."

A priest was running across the square to the church, his skirts flying. He flung himself at the bell rope and pulled it so hard his toes left the ground. The bell that had tolled so slowly and solemnly for my dead grandfather, Nikos Petropoulos, rang out wild and jangling.

Jane put her hands over her ears. She said, half laughing, half frightened, "What a noise! Bad enough, all those women screaming!"

I said, "Olive trees are all some people have got. Their only real income. If they lose the trees, they've lost everything."

The fire was in the valley now, the red smoke swelling up fast toward the village; the smell was bitter and choking, catching the back of the throat. My asthma spray was at the house, in my jacket.

I said, "Mum will be in a state. We'd better go back."

Aliki was still hanging on to my hand. She said, "It'll be *all right*, won't it, Plato? We won't all burn up?"

She sounded much younger than usual: about eight or nine. I said, "Don't be silly, the fire's miles away."

Which it wasn't. The valley was hidden in smoke, but the crackling flames on the mountain beyond it seemed closer. There was nothing to stop them: no firebreaks, no road except the one out of the village. And the wind was getting stronger.

An old truck lurched into the square. It was a cattle truck: open, with high wooden sides. There were a few sheep in it already and more to come; as we started along the path to the house, an old woman came running, driving her white nanny goat, shouting at it and thumping her fist on its back. She chased it into the square and up the ramp of the truck, and when it started skittering backward she went ahead of it, hauling it by its beard. Then she settled herself down beside it.

Jane said, "If they're taking the animals away they must think . . ."

She looked at Aliki and stopped.

I said, "Sheep and goats aren't much help fighting fires."

And laughed, so that Aliki would think I was making a joke. But there was smoke on the other side of the village now. Drifting high above, on the mountain.

My mother and Aunt Elena were hurrying toward us. The big man from next door was with them. Aunt Elena was fastening her black scarf under her chin, fumbling with one hand. She was carrying her handbag. And a picture in a silver frame under her arm. My Greek grandmother's photograph.

"*There* you are!" my mother said, sounding not in the least anxious and no more than ordinarily cross. As if we were just a bit late for supper.

The big man said in English, "The girl will help you at the house, Maria. The young one must go in the truck with Elena. Quickly, while the road is still open."

Aliki looked at him, open-mouthed. Aunt Elena said sharply, "We cannot stay here, Aliki. I am too old and you are too young to be useful."

She put her hand out but Aliki backed away and started to cry, more with temper than fear. "I don't want to go anywhere. I *won't*. Not with a lot of smelly old sheep. I won't go."

She jumped up and down, stamping with both feet in her fury.

Aunt Elena said, "Bring the child, Spiro."

She marched toward the truck without looking back and Spiro picked up Aliki-the-Giantess, it seemed without any effort, and slung her over his shoulder. The truck was already full of old women and children as well as goats and sheep. Aunt Elena was the last up the ramp and it was slammed shut and bolted behind her. Aliki was kicking and screaming and beating Spiro's back with her fists, but he lifted her high over his head and tossed her over the wooden side of the truck as if she were a small baby.

All this happened quicker than it takes to tell. Aliki's scarlet and angry face rearing above the side of the truck as it drove out out of the square; Spiro striding back toward us; and, in that very same moment, one of the tall pencil pines on the edge of the village going up with a *whoosh* like a Roman candle.

I heard my mother gasp. I said, "It must have been an odd spark fell on it, don't worry."

My mother laughed—actually *laughed.* She said, "Don't fuss, Plato. I'm not Aliki! I wonder if you should have gone with her. I should have sent Jane, anyway."

I suppose she meant that it was all right for *me* to be burned to death but she should have taken better care of a visitor!

"I'm not frightened," Jane said. "I'm sure the fire engines will be here soon."

My mother looked at her. "Oh, Jane," she said. "This isn't England."

She suddenly sounded helpless. I said, "I suppose there must be a fire engine in Iria but it would take ages to get here. If it *could* get here, anyway. If the whole valley is burning we may be cut off."

Jane said, "But what do people *do?*" She was looking bewildered.

Spiro said, "They take care themselves." Surprisingly, he was grinning as if Jane had said something funny. He set off along the path to his house and ours, and we followed him.

There was a water tap on the terrace. Spiro filled a tin bucket and hurled the water at the wooden window frames and the door. He said, "You must make everything wet. Soaking. Towels and sheets, anything that will hold water. Watch the fire all round the house, every spark, it must never take hold. Maria, you will show the girl what to do, she can help you. My wife is next door with her sister if you are in trouble."

He looked at me in a calculating way. I stood as tall as I could. It seems stupid now but all I wanted in that dangerous moment was to look old enough.

He made a clicking sound with his tongue. "There is other work for you. First, we go to the square."

◆

It isn't always the important things you remember. People seemed to be running about, here and there, without any obvious purpose, and I thought, *Scuttling like ants*. And then I thought, *Ants know what they're up to!* If you turn over an anthill, they start work at once, mending, repairing, rushing their fat white eggs safe underground . . .

I wish I could say that as I ran after Spiro I was worrying about Jane and my mother, or about Aliki and Aunt Elena, hoping that the road would stay open so the truck could get through and that nothing dreadful would happen, like a burning tree falling on it. But the truth is, all I can really remember is wondering if each ant knew what its job was when the huge spade—huge to *them*—smashed their home open, or if the old ants told the young ants. And I wondered how long ants lived, and I thought how stupid it was not to know something simple like that. And then, how much there was that I didn't know, and if I died now, in this fire, I would die plain pig-ignorant.

I remember thinking that was a silly comparison. Pigs are not especially ignorant. Not as pigs. As pigs, they presumably know all they need to know. But of course the comparison was really between a person and a pig. I ought to know more than a pig.

Of course it only took a second or two for these half-witted thoughts to go through my head, and I only mention them to show how strange it seems that when something really shattering and important is happening, what goes through your mind can be so trivial and irrelevant. Though perhaps other people would have been thinking loftier thoughts about life and death. I can only speak for myself.

And, of course, it didn't stop me doing what I was told to do.

There were men all around the church. Standing ready

with buckets and hoses. Spiro, who seemed to be an important man in the village, started shouting in Greek and some boys, my age and older, came running. They were carrying what looked like broom handles, with long fingers of leather at the end instead of bristles. Someone gave one to me. Spiro said something to them in rapid Greek, then spoke to me in English. "Go with them, where they go, where you see fire. Beat it out, every small spark. It is to keep the road open."

I thought I recognized one of the boys who had thrown stones at Aliki and me on the day of the funeral. As I followed him out of the square, along the road that led out of the village, he gave me a funny look over his shoulder. Half sneer and half smile. But I may have imagined it.

It was almost dark now. I couldn't see the smoke, only smell it, but the fire danced its yellow spikes against the black sky: below us in the valley, above on the mountain, around the whole village.

I thought, *Now I know what it must be like to be in a cannibal's cooking pot.* But I had no more time for further Great Thoughts after that because a spark leapt onto a pile of brushwood at the side of the road and set it alight and I thumped at it with the flail until the last smoldering glint was black ash. And my shoulders were aching.

There were olive trees on the right of the road, the far side from the village, and little fires flickered between them. The boy who had smiled (or sneered) at me jumped the ditch and ran to join other men, black silhouettes against the bright flames, who were thrashing at the fires with wet sacks and heavy spades and whippy green branches. I wondered if I should jump the ditch, too, but this was a crafty fire: skulking behind your back in a line of bright beads or making a sudden dart, like a snake. If I left my patch it might shoot out a sly tongue across the road to the village and set light to a house or a sheepfold.

I thought of Jane and my mother. My grandfather's house, and Spiro's, were at the other end of Molo; there was no road there to act as a firebreak, only the narrow dirt path. I couldn't remember how close the trees came. I wondered if they had remembered to soak the woodpile with water. I coudn't imagine my mother would think of it. Jane was more sensible but she was a town person; she had never lived in a country cottage with a pile of wood stacked by the door ready for winter. And the wood would be dry after the long, dusty summer.

By this time I was off the road, in the ditch, beating back the sneaky little flames from the olive grove. The boy next to me was coughing as if he might be sick in a minute. I was a bit wheezy with the smoke but not as much as I would have expected. The worst thing was the heat, especially around the rims of my glasses. I thought, *My eyeballs will melt!*

Someone shouted among the olive trees and the men began running back. Two of the trees themselves were on fire. Then a third. They made a brilliant blaze, yellow and white at the edges. I scrambled out of the ditch, back to the road, and almost fell under the wheels of a van full of children that was clattering slowly past, its rear doors swinging, held roughly together by string. Behind the van, and almost keeping pace with it, a tiny old nun was pushing a wheelbarrow load of things from the church—I could see the silver frame of an icon and the shine of brass.

For about thirty seconds I looked after her, watching her

busy little feet in running shoes going like clockwork under her habit. Then there was a great solid *whumph*—like a bomb going off. One of the blazing olive trees had burst open. The men who had been fighting the fires in the grove were back on the road now, and, as the tree exploded, splitting in pieces and shooting sparks into the dark sky like a huge firework, they began groaning together.

It wasn't funny, of course it wasn't in the least funny. But I wanted to laugh all the same, hearing all those men wailing and moaning like the chorus in an Ancient Greek play. I thought, *Laugh or cry, it doesn't change anything.* And that made me stop wanting to laugh at once because it seemed so terrible that once something had happened like this, like the olive trees burning, nothing anyone did—or felt, or thought, or said—could make any difference.

The boy who had jumped the ditch to join the men in the grove was sniveling beside me, holding out burned, swollen hands. I said, "Go and put them in water," and he looked at me blankly, tears and snot and soot running down his blackened face, and I said, "Oh, I can't speak Greek, I'm so sorry." Then I remembered the word for water and said it. "*Nero,*" I said. "*Nero.*"

I don't know whether he understood me even then. I would like to be able to say that I fetched a bucket of water and saved his hands from being damaged forever—if he could have been a violinist or a surgeon that would have made an even better story—but the truth is that any water around at that moment would have gone on the olive trees and not on someone's burned hands. The whole grove was alight and all that could be done now was to try and stop the fire crossing the road and cutting Molo off from the outside world altogether.

◆

I don't know if this was something I understood then or if I worked it out later. What I do remember is that the fire in the olive grove had got so fierce that we had to back away, shielding our faces, and then, suddenly, a bit farther on, just before the T-junction beyond the village, a long, coiling, dragon's lick shot across the road and lit dancing sparks in the thorny hedge on the other side. Only a few, but they were close to some houses.

We all started running but the bulldozer passed us. Spiro was driving; he had a white cloth tied around his head that covered his forehead and eyes. When he got to the junction, he swiveled the bulldozer round, making an oily grinding and squealing sound loud enough to be heard above the roar of the fire, and drove it straight at the burning olive grove. Straight into the heart of the fire.

The first olive tree went down with a splintering crack. Spiro stopped, reversed the bulldozer, and drove forward again at another tree. Backward and forward, backward and forward, widening and deepening the firebreak with every thrust, working his way back from the main road toward the village.

He was covered in splinters of fire. A woman came running with a wet towel and he stopped just long enough to wrap it around his nose and his mouth. Then he charged forward again, backward and forward without stopping, going at it as if he were an engine himself. Or a madman.

Or a hero. It was the bravest thing I had ever seen. I thought, *I will remember it all my life! When people talk about brave deeds I will remember Spiro driving into the flames on his bulldozer and have something to judge them by.*

◆

It made all of us on the road a bit braver, too. Although the boy with burned hands disappeared, the rest of us followed the bulldozer and thumped away at the firebreak Spiro was making until it was black, beaten ash, not a trace of fire, even when we kicked at it. There was still a risk of stray sparks blowing over the road, but the hedges and the houses on the other side had been soaked with water and the women and the older men were on guard. Watching them, I began to worry about Jane and my mother.

When Spiro got down from the bulldozer, his boots were on fire! There was a line of red light trickling between the soles and the uppers! Another man drove the bulldozer away while Spiro stamped his feet up and down and banged them sideways against tufts of charred grass. Then he sat on a low stone wall, still keeping an eye on his boots and wiping his face and neck with a grimy towel. He had kept the road open, but no one paid him any attention or seemed to think he had done anything special; one man stayed, sitting on the wall beside him and smoking a cigarette, but everyone else began to drift away, back toward the square. I hung around for a bit, but there was nothing obvious to do and Spiro was in no state to give orders, so I followed the others.

The square was crowded with sheep as well as people. The sheep were making a terrible hullabaloo, baa-ing away in an indignant sort of way. *You humans ought to know that this is not how we expect to be treated!* The church had been on fire, you could smell it, but it looked safe enough now; a couple of nuns were folding a hose in the porch and looking as calm as if they had been watering flowers in the garden.

◆

Trying to describe something like this kind of huge fire is difficult for someone who was actually there. One person can only have seen a part of what happened. It must be like being in the middle of a battle; a general, watching from a high hill, might know if his side is winning or losing, but all an ordinary soldier can see is the other soldier next to him having his leg blown off.

I'll do my best. To start with, there was this thick, choking smell. And the heat. And the people shouting and crying and running. And the crackling flames shooting up against the dark sky. And the olive trees exploding because of the oil in their trunks and the pine trees shooting like rockets into the sky. The people of Molo had fought the fire from the beginning, to keep it away from the village, and were still fighting hours later, but they couldn't go on forever, and if help didn't come soon, firefighting planes or fire engines or a miracle like a rainstorm, we would all be burned to death at the end.

It was funny, I thought, that I wasn't more frightened. Then I thought, *My mother must be scared out of her wits.* Most nights she couldn't even bear to watch the news on the television.

I started running at once. The track that led from the square to my grandfather's house was surprisingly empty and quiet, no sign of fire. I ran past the house where the white nanny goat lived, the one that had gone in the same truck as Aliki, and saw that someone had hung heavy wet sacks over the windows and doorway and that water glinted in the buckets that stood on the stone terrace. Then I heard someone screaming.

My grandfather's house looked safe and the house next door, Spiro's house, looked the same: deepest dark, no lights—of course, because the electricity had gone ages ago—and no sign of fire. It was down the mountain, where the land fell steeply away below my grandfather's terraced garden, that the bright flames were leaping.

I had never noticed a house there before. It was such a little house, a couple of thorn trees and a few scraggy bushes had been enough to hide it. Now they had burned down, the hut could be seen: fire licking around it, black shadows dancing against it, and an old woman sitting on the ground rocking backward and forward and from time to time letting out a piercing metallic scream. A bit like a peacock.

There was a way down to the little house, a stony goat track more than a path. As I slid down it, I saw that my mother and Jane were among the black shadows fighting the fire. They looked as if they had been rolling in soot. I was so glad to see them I could have hugged them if they had given me time. But my mother said, *"There* you are, Plato!"—as if I had been deliberately dawdling. And Jane, "Get some *water*. Buckets on the terrace. Help Spiro's wife!"

They were both banging away with heavy wet sacks that seemed more effective than the flail I'd been using, but I guessed they were very much heavier. As I raced back up the mountain I thought my mother must have discovered some strange new reserve of muscular strength. She always *claimed* she couldn't carry a suitcase! Or the shopping home from the supermarket!

I met Mrs. Spiro halfway up. Or Mrs. Spiro's sister. A stout person, triangular in shape, with a face that was brown and lined as a walnut. She had a slopping-over bucket in each hand; she handed them both to me and went stumping back up on legs that were thick and solid as tree trunks. She must have been strong as an elephant. *My* legs buckled under the weight of those buckets and I felt that my arms were being torn from my shoulders.

I got them down all the same and they were seized at once by a small, bent, and wrinkled old man who flung the first bucket of water at the fire, which hissed and trembled very nicely. I was about to do the same with the second bucket when he jerked his head back up the mountain and I saw that my job was to be bucket-carrier.

"Don't they have *hoses?*" I said to Jane, as I ran past her.

She didn't answer, but my mother gave a wild shriek and came racing past me, beating me up the slope, pushing past Mrs. Spiro (or her sister), almost knocking her over and almost spilling her water. I followed her and found her crouching in a patch of thistles behind my grandfather's woodpile, muttering to herself, "Years ago . . . I should have remembered . . ."

The hose had been a good strong one once but it was very old now. The night seemed less dark suddenly and we could see rips in it and the end was frayed. I thrust the hose onto the tap as firmly as I could while my mother uncoiled it as she slipped and slid down the steep stony path. When she shouted up to me, I turned on the tap and the hose twisted and juddered like a sleeping snake come to life. I could hear cries from below and the hiss of the fire but I couldn't leave the tap; the hose was splitting as the water gushed through it, and holding it was the hardest *physical* thing I had ever done. Each time I was sure I would have to let go, that I couldn't possibly hold the hose firm any longer, I wrapped my hands tighter around it.

I remembered a story about a boy with his hand in a hole in the dike. But that was in Holland. And he was trying to hold the water back, not make sure it kept coming.

I couldn't tell what was happening to the burning house because the hill beyond it was still bright with fire. It seemed to be lighting the sky. When Jane came to tell me they had put the fire out, I said, "It isn't as dark as it was."

She said, "You half-wit. It's morning. The house is all right. Not burning, anyway. They don't need any more water."

I tried to turn the tap off but my fingers were too clawed and stiff. I couldn't move them.

As Jane did it for me, I said, plantively, "I shall never play the violin again." Then, because she didn't laugh, "It can't really be *morning!*"

"About four o'clock." She was yawning.

"But it started at *sunset.*"

She said, "Not so long, really. About seven hours. You look filthy!"

I stood up. I was cramped up like a very old man. I crept to the edge of the terrace on crooked legs and looked at the smoking ruin of the little house. The stone walls were still standing but there wasn't much left of the rest of it. I said, "Poor old woman."

"At least she's not burned to death." Jane pulled a face. "Not yet, anyway."

I saw how frightened she suddenly was. She had been fighting her own small bit of the fire. Now she had time to think about the rest of it. What was going to happen.

I said, "Spiro kept the road open. So they can get a fire engine through. If there *is* a fire engine. Or we'll just have to keep on trying to keep it away from the village. Until it dies down by itself."

Not much hope of that, I thought. A fire like this could burn for days. We would run out of water. It was astonishing that we hadn't already.

We stood on the terrace and watched the mountains burning. The village was safe for the moment but we were completely circled by a ring of flames, leaping and spurting around us. As if the fire was threatening and teasing us. Waiting its chance to destroy us. I wondered how long it would take.

I said, a bit desperately, "I suppose you could say that it's beautiful. A sort of firework display. Only a bit too end-of-the-worldish."

I tried to think of something else cheerful to say but there didn't seem to be anything. My thought about being bubbled up in a cannibal's cooking pot seemed too near the bone to be funny. Jane moved close to me and sighed. I took her hand and she drew in her breath with pain. Her hands were scarlet and blistered.

That was something to do, at least. I made her put her

hands under the tap. She made a bit of a fuss but she kept them there.

My mother's voice startled us. She said, "We may need that water."

People were coming up from the little stone house, among them the old woman it must belong to, the one who had screamed like a peacock. My mother had her arm round her shoulders.

I said, "Jane's hands are burned," but my mother paid no attention. She was looking up at the path, at Spiro who was striding toward us. He was waving his arms and shouting in Greek, then he turned and ran back. My mother gasped, and laughed. Then she started shouting—also in Greek, of course—and everyone on the terrace began laughing too, and thumping each other.

Jane and I stood there, bewildered. My mother turned to us, laughing and crying together. She said, "Oh, my darlings, you're safe. The army is coming."

⊛CHAPTER·12

The army came, and the water planes, dropping seawater on the forest fires.

I saw the water planes, flying as low as they could over the mountains, because they came and went all the next day until all the fires were out. But I missed the arrival of the army trucks with their water cannons because I was asleep. There was nothing much for them to do, anyway. Although my mother said everyone cheered when the army rumbled into the square, the villagers had already saved Molo themselves. With a little help from some of us foreigners who happened to be there.

Jane and I went to sleep without washing, and in our torn, dirty clothes. I don't actually remember going up the stairs to the attic, or in fact anything, but my mother must have put some stuff on our burns because when I woke I could see two huge, white, bandaged hands sticking out of Jane's sleeping bag.

I slithered out of my bag quiet as I could and went downstairs. My clothes smelt—*I* smelt—quite horrible. A harsh, bitter smell.

It wasn't just me, it was everywhere. In the air. The kind of smell that catches the back of your throat. My mother was sitting on the terrace with a cup of coffee in her hands and when I came out, holding my nose, she put it down, shaking her head. She said, "It gets into everything. Even into the coffee."

She had washed and changed her clothes but she looked very strange because her hair was burned off on one side. Just a few dry spikes left. She saw me looking and put her hands up and said, "Is it so awful?"

She couldn't have seen how bad it really was. My grandfather had not been a vain man. There was only one looking glass in the house, in the bathroom, and that was so high up that my mother would have had to stand on the lavatory seat to look into it. I said, "I don't suppose any of us would exactly qualify for a beauty competition just at that moment. But if you don't want to frighten Aliki you'd better put a scarf on."

I thought I had better not mention Tasso.

"Oh, well," she said. "It'll grow."

I thought that was a bit *hardy* coming from her. She always fussed so much over her appearance, sometimes changing her clothes half a dozen times before she went out in the evening.

She said, "We might have died, Plato. Everyone. The whole village." She sounded calm. Almost *smug*.

I said, "We could have left, couldn't we? In the truck with Aliki."

"I should have sent Jane. It was none of her business," my mother said—rather oddly I thought, but before I could ask what she meant, she went on. "Though Jane was quite *wonderful*. A real heroine. She didn't give up for a minute. I couldn't have managed without her."

"I would have stayed with you if she hadn't been there." It was nice to hear her say Jane was wonderful but I was a bit miffed all the same, for some reason. I said, "I'll have a bath. I don't think there's any point in keeping these clothes, do you? They wouldn't even be much use to a scarecrow."

I thought if she took a good look at my scorched and tattered garments she would realize that I had been pretty busy last night, just as busy as Jane. But she only glanced casually at me and said, "The water's turned off. Luckily we still have a bit left in the buckets. Just leave some for Jane."

I said, "How come the water's off now? It kept going last night."

"I imagine the men who look after the pump needed their sleep. It can't have been an easy night for them."

I thought she spoke sharply, as if this might be partly *my* fault, but perhaps I imagined it because she suddenly turned motherly, fetching my spare set of clothes while I sluiced myself down with an economical third of a bucket of water, and tenderly examining the burns on my arms—which were not very bad, to be honest!

And then, when I was dressed and felt all at once very hungry, she said she would find me some breakfast. There was the bread and butter and milk we had brought from Iria but we couldn't cook anything; the kitchen worked on electricity and there was no power now in the village. Unfortunately my stomach craved fried eggs.

"Some people will be all right, the ones who have old baking ovens or open fires," my mother said, and, as if by magic, just at that moment, Mrs. Spiro—I wondered if I should ever know if she was Spiro's wife or Spiro's wife's sister—appeared at the top of our steps with a tray. She lumbered down, beaming, and set it down on the table in front of me.

"You must have read my mind," I said, looking down at a plate that had four perfect fried eggs on it, the whites crisp and curling but the yellow yolks ready to burst at the touch of a fork. I spoke in English but my meaning must have got through to her because she cackled happily.

"She's been watching for you ever since she brought me my coffee," my mother said when she had gone. "There's nothing Greek women like better than feeding young men."

I was going to point out that no one had behaved in such a neighborly way the last time we had been in Molo, but then I thought better of it, not wanting conversation to hold up closer acquaintance with the fried eggs. And then my mother went off to wake Jane, and after that the water planes came, and we sat watching them droning over the thick pall of reddish smoke that hung over the mountains and dropping their cargoes of sea water.

I told Jane about the fried eggs, and the friendliness. I said, "After what happened last time, I hadn't expected it."

"I expect it was the fire," Jane said. "An emergency is bound to make people friendly. They have to depend on one another. And your mother was *wonderful* last night. She looks so little, and sort of breakable, but she flew at the fire like a *tiger*."

She had said "wonderful" in exactly the same rapturous

tone my mother had used about her. I pointed out that tigers were not normally noted for their firefighting skills but all I got in return for this pearl of wisdom and wit was a deeply reproachful look.

"Your mum got that old woman out of her house when no one else could get her to budge! She went in to fetch her, though the roof was already *burning* and might have fallen in on them both!"

◆

Human nature is very peculiar. I was proud—as well as astonished—that my mother had turned out so brave. All the same, I found the mutual admiration society that she and Jane had set up together somewhat annoying.

Well, of course, I hadn't been asked to join. I said things like, "It was really hard work keeping the road open." And, "Spiro was jolly brave, driving the bulldozer straight at the fire, but it wouldn't have worked if the rest of us hadn't kept on beating the firebreak behind him."

They listened politely but I could tell they weren't interested. All they cared about was what had happened in their bit of the fire, as if nothing that had gone on in another part of the village could have been really important. And since there were two of them, each able to witness how "wonderful" the other had been, I was rather left out of things.

Even my war wounds were not as dramatic as theirs. Although my mother had hidden her hairless skull under a scarf, there was a nasty red mark down the side of her face. And Jane's hands meant she was more or less crippled. She couldn't hold a glass of milk or eat a slice of bread and honey, so I had to feed her. It would have been a fine opportunity to tease her a bit, but she looked so pale that I knew her burns must be hurting her.

I said, "I wish I could take the pain off. I'd have it myself if I could."

I almost meant this, not quite but *almost*, and she knew this exactly. She said "Thank you," very nicely but with a bit of an evil grin, so I knew she was still in the world of the living, and when my mother said Jane must stay and rest on the terrace while she and I went to the square to see if anyone needed help, I didn't mind leaving her.

"Though I don't know what sort of use we're likely to be," I objected as my mother and I set off down the path.

"There are a lot of old people in Molo. They can't all clean up their own houses. There'll be a lot of rubbish, dust and dirt, the sort of thing the army won't do for them and nobody else will take care of."

I didn't believe a word of this. She had rattled it off much too quickly. And even if she had behaved bravely last night, that didn't mean she had suddenly become a different person, someone who was thirsting to get down on her hands and knees and scrub some old person's stone floor.

No! My mother had some private game of her own! She had glanced at me once, a quick, guilty look; after that she kept her gaze fixed on distance. And I was beginning to feel very uneasy. Last night was last night, after all. We had been extra hands to fight the fire. Today was another thing altogether.

I began to feel my flesh crawl. We had almost got to the square. I said, "Mum, let's go back. You know what it was like last time. When we came for the funeral. Let's go back to the house and wait for Aunt Elena. She's bound to come,

[158]

isn't she? Soon as she can get a lift. Or a taxi to take us all back to Iria."

She didn't pay attention. It was as if she hadn't heard me. She walked firmly on and I had to follow her. I couldn't leave her to run the gauntlet alone.

People were sitting at the cafés and under the plane tree. They looked grubby, rumpled, and weary. There was only one child there, one small boy left behind, playing alone with his little bike and singing under his breath. My mother stopped to speak to him as we crossed the square and he hung his head shyly.

At the first café she said, "*Yassas*," smiling, and to my surprise, to my utter relief and amazement, half a dozen people got up to greet her, shaking her hand or embracing her. She turned to me then, introducing me in Greek, and my hand was shaken and my cheeks kissed as well. Not everyone had managed to wash after the fire and some of them smelled pretty pungent.

After that we made a kind of royal progress around the square. I guessed that a lot of questions were being asked, and my mother jabbered away in answer, but as it was all in Greek I had no idea what was actually said, although I guessed it must be some kind of elaborate greeting ritual since the same words were repeated over and over. *How are you? How is your family? This is your son? And your daughter, how is she? What does your husband do? How much does he earn?*

The Greeks go in for this sort of thing rather more than the English, who tend to mumble at each other and think it is rude to talk about money.

When we had pressed the last hand, kissed the last cheek,

[159]

my mother said, "I think we shouldn't leave Jane alone any longer."

Her cheeks were flushed; her brown eyes dancing.

I said, as we walked back along the path, "I don't understand, Mum."

She laughed, but in an embarrassed way. "I can't explain, Plato. It's too—oh, I don't know—I just think you would think it too silly."

"Try me, Mum. Is it because we helped fight the fire?"

"In a sort of way. That's not the whole of it and I don't think I can really explain it. It's to do with my father. Just that all is well with him now."

And that was all she would say.

◆

It was Tasso who explained what she meant, in the end. He came late in the afternoon, not in the Mercedes but in a big Mitsubishi Space Wagon, bringing back some of the children who had been sent to safety the night before. Aliki was with them. I thought she would be furious with our mother and me, but she was bursting with pride and excitement because Tasso had asked her to help him with the little ones. And there was something else, too. "I know something you don't," she said, looking slyly at me as we all sat on the terrace drinking beautiful, cold lemonade that Aunt Elena had made and sent in a thermos with Tasso.

"That'll do, Princess," Tasso said automatically. As usual, he was watching my mother. She was wearing her scarf but it had slipped back a bit and, suddenly, she gave an impatient sigh and pulled it off altogether. She looked straight at Tasso and smiled. She said, "Now you know what I'll look like when I'm old and bald, so you can change your mind if you want to."

He rushed at her then, putting his arms round her, kissing her bald patch and telling her not to worry, it would soon grow again, and generally carrying on in the kind of doting way that makes other people who are forced to look on wish they could summon a genie and be transported elsewhere immediately. The only thing that remotely interested me in this soppy scene was how little fuss my mother was making over what she would have once thought a simply huge tragedy.

Perhaps she had changed more than I thought, after all.

◆

When Tasso had finished patting and pawing my mother, it was possible to have a conversation and make sensible plans. Tasso was to drive us all back to Iria in the afternoon, which would give my mother time to leave her father's house tidy. In the meantime, Tasso had arranged to take some of the men from the village to look at the damage the fire had done to their olive trees up the mountain.

"You will come with me, Plato," he said. "Aliki will help her mother."

Giving us no option, as usual. But Aliki didn't seem to mind and I didn't mind as much as I once would have done. Besides, in this case the alternative appeared to be house-work, for which I am not temperamentally suited.

In the square, the Space Wagon filled up with grim-faced men. I sat in the front with Tasso. No one said much as we turned off the paved road onto a ridged track that led steeply up and around the mountain. From time to time one of the men in the back muttered softly or groaned.

It was worse than I could have imagined. Everywhere and everything had burned. The olive trees rose like shadows out of the bare ground, their charred trunks torn and twisted. Here and there a patch of green remained on one side of a blackened stump, a few shriveled gray leaves. The smell of burning was thick in the air.

Tasso stopped. He turned off the engine. The men got out of the back and set off into the devastated olive groves, some in pairs, some alone, all in silence.

Tasso said, "This is a terrible moment for them. Each of their trees will be known. Like their children."

I said, "What started the fire?"

"A match. A worn electric cable." Tasso frowned, tapping his fingers on the steering wheel as if counting the possibilities. He said, "There are fewer people nowadays who collect the brushwood for fires, and that means the forests catch fire more easily. Sometimes it is deliberate. Arson. Someone demonstrating against the government."

One of the men had thrown himself on the ground and was banging his head up and down. He was howling, as if he was in great pain.

Tasso said, "I have something to tell you, Plato. I hope it will please you."

It seemed wrong to watch the man in the olive grove— wrong to *want* to watch him!—but I couldn't help it. It felt like a kind of greediness. I actually felt odd and empty in my stomach and the saliva came up in my mouth.

I tried to be sorry for him. I tried to think about his life, to wonder if he had a family to feed this next winter and how he would do it. Then he got up from the ground and brushed the ashy dirt off his knees and I gave up trying to ignore what Tasso was telling me.

Which was, of course, that he was going to marry my mother.

He wanted to know how I felt about it. I couldn't think of an intelligent answer. He said that Aliki seemed pleased enough.

I thought, *I bet she was pleased! Another source of rich presents!*

"I'm not *not* pleased," I snarled. "Just that it's a surprise."

Lying in my teeth. And with my usual charm and grace! I would have had to be blind and brainless and deaf as a post not to have noticed that they didn't exactly hate each other.

I managed to spit out something about hoping they would be happy, though I fear it may have sounded as if my hopes lay in quite another direction. Tasso bound to a rock with ants crawling all over him and my mother locked up in a nunnery.

Though that wasn't what I felt, really. I mean, I didn't give a hoot for Tasso's feelings. But I wanted *her* to be happy.

Tasso said, "Good. I hope we will all get on well together. There is no reason why we should not."

I added, silently, *As long as you do what you're told!* But perhaps that was unfair to him. He was beaming, very pleased with himself, and with me. He said, "I have loved your mother since we were students together. I have waited for her ever since. No other girl could have taken her place. She is a unique person."

Yuck! I was terrified! The thought of having to listen to

this sort of emotional drivel until the villagers returned from mourning their olive trees, for the next *half hour*, probably, almost paralyzed my vocal cords. Almost, but not quite. In a sort of strangled squeak, I managed to produce, as an example of my mother's uniqueness, her peculiar behavior this morning. "What I don't understand," I croaked, "is what it had to do with her *father*."

Tasso was quiet for what seemed a long time but was maybe only a minute. Time is peculiar. In the way that the six or seven hours we were fighting the fire seemed much shorter, the silence while I waited for Tasso to answer went on for ages.

At last he said, "You know how the people of Molo felt about your grandfather. He was buried with many sins on him. But for a Greek, the good deeds of a child, or a grandchild, can sometimes lighten a burden. When a Greek is dug up after five years in the grave and his bones are white and clean, it means he is at last free from sin. Last night, you and your mother fought for the village. That will have helped to whiten your grandfather's bones."

I said, "But that's *horrible*. I mean, it's superstitious and *disgusting!*"

"You may prefer to think that your hard work last night merely restored your grandfather's reputation," Tasso said. "But it is not quite the same thing."

"I'm sure it's how my mother thinks of it." I thought, *Now answer that one!*

"Maria is very Greek," Tasso said. "So I doubt it."

"I think being Greek is stupid." As soon as I had said this I knew I sounded childish. So I went on hastily, "I mean, if it makes you believe such primitive nonsense."

[164]

I was so angry that I banged with my fists on the dashboard.

Tasso laughed. "You're quite Greek yourself. Waving your hands about."

"I don't *want* to be," I said, scowling. This sounded so rude, I had to explain to him that it was being half and half that I found so difficult. Feeling Greek in England and Wales, and English in Greece. "I just don't belong anywhere," I said. "I live in England, but I'm not English, I'm bits of Greek, bits of Welsh. I'm not a *whole person!*"

"Would you like to be the same all through? Like a bowl of porridge?"

I shook my head. Tasso looked at me gravely. "You have to be yourself, I think. That is harder than belonging to a tribe but better in the end because you can be at home everywhere. A Citizen of the World."

◆

That was the end of that conversation, because the men began to come straggling back at that moment and Tasso gave them his whole attention, as was only polite.

And it was really the end of this story. Because although many things happened afterward, they all followed on from the things I have written down here. My mother and I sold the flat and some of the furniture and packed up the things she wanted to take with her when she and Tasso were married. Tasso has a house in Athens and one in Paris and an apartment in New York. He would like Aliki and me to go to boarding school (there is a school in Switzerland he is particularly keen on) and spend the holidays with him and my mother wherever they happen to be. But for the moment,

[165]

in term time, Aliki is still with our father (and the Dentist-Doll and the Dentist-Doll's baby daughter) and I am staying with Jane and her aunts, with Aunt Bill and Aunt Sophie, which suits me much better than shooting about from one place to the other, and means that I can stay at my school and continue to enrage our stupid headmaster for a little while longer. And I have more time to argue with Jane.

My mother gets more Greek by the minute. Not because of Tasso; I have noticed it growing in her since the night of the fire. And in fact I have been feeling more Greek myself since I saw the olive trees burning. But I can put on a Welsh accent that would fool even a Welshman. I have even learned a few words of Welsh to please my old grandmother. And of course, at school I am as English as Jane.

But none of this bothers me any longer. When people ask me my name it is easy to answer them. I am Plato Constantine Jones: Plato because of Nikos Petropoulos and Constantine because of CLJ. Everyone has heard about CLJ, but I sometimes have to explain that Nikos Petropoulos was just as brave and that I am just as proud of him. I aim to be a World Citizen. In the meantime, both my grandfathers fit very comfortably inside my own skin.

About the Author

There is no better storyteller than Nina Bawden. "With miraculous skill, Bawden places yet another set of vibrant characters in a compelling plot seasoned with cold reality, the warmth of enduring relationships, and moral ironies," began the *Kirkus Reviews'* description of her most recent book, *Humbug*. Those same words could be said about any book Nina Bawden writes.

Bawden says about writing for children: "I may be a grownup now, but I am also, simultaneously and pervasively, a former child. Running alongside, keeping me company always, is a much younger person; a rather fat little girl, a spy and a liar by nature, inquisitive, sharp-eyed, and often quite rude. If I fall into the ordinary grownup trap of indifference to, which can mean contempt *for*, a child's understanding and experience, that fat little girl is there to haul me out of it."

Nina Bawden and her husband, Austen Kark, divide their time between their homes in London and Greece. They have traveled widely throughout the world. They chose Greece for a second home after spending much time there and coming to know its people and customs well.